MUCHACHO

MUCHACHO

A NOVEL

LOUANNE JOHNSON

EMBER

Text copyright © 2009 by LouAnne Johnson
Cover photograph © by Shutterstock

All rights reserved. Published in the United States by Ember,
an imprint of Random House Children's Books, a division of Random House, Inc., New York.
Originally published in hardcover in the United States by Alfred A. Knopf, an imprint of
Random House Children's Books, a division of Random House, Inc., New York, in 2009.

Ember and the colophon are trademarks of Random House, Inc.

Visit us on the Web! www.randomhouse.com/teens

Educators and librarians, for a variety of teaching tools,
visit us at www.randomhouse.com/teachers

The Library of Congress has cataloged the hardcover edition of this work as follows:
Johnson, LouAnne.
Muchacho / LouAnne Johnson. —1st American ed.
p.   cm.
Summary: Living in a neighborhood of drug dealers and gangs in New Mexico,
high school junior Eddie Corazon, a juvenile delinquent-in-training, falls in love
with a girl who inspires him to rethink his life and his choices.
ISBN 978-0-375-86117-8 (trade) — ISBN 978-0-375-96117-5 (lib. bdg.) —
ISBN 978-0-375-89355-1 (ebook)
[1. Self-perception—Fiction. 2. Mexican Americans—Fiction. 3. High School—Fiction.
4. Schools—Fiction. 5. New Mexico—Fiction.] I. Title.
PZ7.J6325Mu 2009
[Fic]—dc22
2009001768

ISBN 978-0-375-85903-8 (pbk.)

RL: 9.3

Printed in the United States of America

10 9 8

First Ember Edition 2011

For Corey, who never meant to kick that teacher

and for all the "secret readers"
who are sitting in school
keeping their intelligence to themselves

CHAPTER 1

BEECHER AT THE LIBRARY

I SEEN MISS BEECHER TODAY AT THE LIBRARY CHECKING OUT A old lady's book. She had her head tipped down so I couldn't see her face real good but I knew it was Beecher on account of her hair is the exact same color as a car I stole once. Bronze metallic. Beecher doesn't look like a regular librarian but at least she didn't look like she was falling off a cliff the way she did most of the time back when she was trying to be a teacher.

I didn't go all the way inside the library, just stood in the doorway waiting for Letty and Juanito to finish listening to the story lady, but Juanito saw me and he yelled, "Eddie!" I quick looked at Beecher to see if she heard Juanito holler my name because if Beecher looked at me, then I would nod, maybe say, "Hey, how's it going." But she was busy helping another old lady find her library card so I ducked out.

First time I saw Beecher, I thought, Oh great, another one of those Peace Corps people with their organic shoes and their tofu sandwiches and their posters showing how important it is to save the whales and the rain forests and the baby seals and me and all the other semi-literate at-risk underprivileged economically deprived youth at the alt school who don't really give a shit about getting an education because what difference would it make if we did. We'd still be us. We'd still be freaks and losers except we'd be freaks and losers with educations, so we'd understand exactly what we couldn't have.

The day Beecher showed up at our English class, Edgar Martinez asked how long had she been a teacher. We knew Beecher was virgin the second she started to answer the question because the old teachers know better than to leave themselves open like that. Beecher told us she was going through a program for alternative certification because she didn't decide to become a teacher until after she already graduated college. So she said we had something in common because she was an alternative teacher and we were alternative students. For like two seconds, I started to fall for that idea, but I caught myself in time.

I don't miss Beecher or nothing, but at least she was better than the guy we have now who is a total pathetic pussy who wears pink glasses. He thinks if he tells us four hundred times a day that he went to Stanford University, then we'll appreciate what a big sacrifice he's making to be a teacher who gets paid crap and works in a place that looks worser than Juárez. He thinks we'll like him for devoting his life to helping disadvantaged kids become successful, productive members of society but we mostly think he's a *pinche* dickhead. At least if he was driving around in a cool car with a hot stereo and a shiny rich girl in the jump seat, we could be jealous and hate him and maybe we would jack him up and take his car, but now we hate him worser because he could of had all that stuff and he was too stupid to take it, so now nobody has it. If he really wanted to help kids who didn't have his advantages, he could of saved up his giant allowance and got his parents to buy him a real expensive car and then he could of just came here and gave us the money and the car. He could of even sold lottery tickets. I bet a lot of kids would go to school if they might win twenty bucks or a car just for showing up. But he blew it. How can you respect a teacher who wasn't even smart enough to figure that out?

Beecher didn't try to pretend she didn't appreciate her nice easy white-girl life. And she wasn't scared of us like most of the lady teachers are even though she's skinny enough that you could probably pick her up and throw her down the stairs real easy. And she didn't try to feed us all that crap about how useful our education was going to be someday, like how we would need algebra to figure out how many square feet of carpet we need in our living room because everybody knows that we'll be renting some crappy apartment our whole life and even if we could buy a house, measuring the carpet is the carpet guy's job and he probably has a calculator.

The first day when nobody would open their grammar books to the page number she wrote on the board, Beecher didn't even yell. She just sat down on the edge of her desk, still holding her book, and looked around the room. Not with mean eyes. More like she was surprised that we weren't all following her. Like if a mother duck turned around and instead of waddling along in that nice neat little line, the baby ducks were running all over the place where they could get lost or killed so easy.

"Wouldn't it make more sense to exert a little effort and get through this material quickly, so we can move on to something more interesting and relevant to your lives?" Beecher asked us.

"Oh yeah. Ha!" T.J. Ritchie laughed his hard dirty laugh. "Like how to sell more crack?" T.J. is big, really big, probably seven feet tall, and he doesn't give a shit about anything. Usually new teachers give T.J. that look that says you're a stupid nothing loser and someday you'll be sorry you wasted your pitiful little life. Or they send him to the office or else just ignore him, but Beecher hooked her hair behind her ear with her finger like she does when she's thinking and said, "You're a drug dealer?"

T.J. shook his head and made check-her-out faces at his friends and they were all like, Duh. Beecher walked over and opened the door. "Then you might as well go." She flung her arm out into the hallway.

"You can't kick me out," T.J. said. "I didn't do nothing."

"I'm not kicking you out," Beecher said. "I want you to stay. But if you want to be a criminal, I can't help you."

"I don't need your help, lady. You think you're all better than us but you're not."

"I absolutely do not believe I am better than you." Beecher shook her head and her hair sort of shimmered around her ears. "I can understand perfectly well how a person might decide to reject capitalism and corporate corruption and choose a criminal career over a traditional education."

By this time, T.J. and everybody else was just staring at Beecher like she needed to get real, but she kept on talking. Her voice is thick and smooth like a talk show lady and she has this way of saying stuff that sticks in your brain afterwards and plays back even when you aren't thinking about it, like those TV commercials that get stuck in your head and drive you *loco*.

"You and I have different ethics and values, Mr. Ritchie," Beecher said. "I choose to live within the law because I could never survive being incarcerated, but if you don't mind risking your freedom in pursuit of a life that offers you fulfillment, that is your choice. However, analyzing literature will not help you be a more successful drug dealer, which is why I suggest that if you seriously wish to pursue that avenue, you focus your efforts on your criminal career. The sooner you start, the better chance you have of being successful—until you are incarcerated or killed."

5

T.J. didn't say anything for a minute and he probably would have let it slide except this one girl giggled, so he had to say, "Whatever." Then I think Beecher realized you should never talk that long to a kid like T.J. because she closed the door real quiet and folded her arms and looked around at the rest of us.

"That goes for everybody," she said. "If you truly didn't want to be here, you wouldn't be. And I am not foolish enough to think I can make you do anything. So we won't even pretend that you have to do the assignments. And I would prefer not to have this discussion again."

We didn't have that discussion again, but we had a lot of other ones that the school board wouldn't have liked even though they are usually pretty desperate for teachers because New Mexico is like forty-nine out of fifty when it comes to how dumb and fucked-up the students are and how backwards the school board is and how fast the teachers give up and go away. If we lived in one of those smart states like New York or California, there would probably be a whole lot of teachers like Beecher, and she wouldn't even have to worry about getting fired for being a liberal intellectual.

One thing about Beecher I remember the most is that she would look you right in the eye when she was talking to you and you could tell she wasn't thinking bad things about you, even if you just said something real stupid or pronounced a word wrong when you were reading out loud. Like if you were reading something about trains and you said DEE-POT instead of DEE-POE, she wouldn't let anybody laugh at you. She would just wait until you were done reading and then she would say, "Has anybody ever been to a train depot?" and she would pronounce it the right way to let you know how you were supposed to say it. The other teachers would jump on that wrong word and pronounce it the right way the second you said it wrong because even though they went to college and we didn't, they always have to show how smart they are. But Beecher was too busy trying to show us how smart we were instead of how smart she was, so by the time we wised up to how smart she was, she was already gone.

CHAPTER 2

GETTING RID OF A TEACHER

AT BRIGHT HORIZONS, IT'S PRETTY EASY TO GET RID OF A teacher. All you got to do is get a few kids to pretend the teacher inspired you to turn over a new leaf and live up to your potential and appreciate the opportunity to get a free education. That teacher will get so psyched about being your mentor and role model that they'll answer any questions you ask them, even if you slip in a question about evolution or gay marriage. Then you pretend like you just love going to school because you're learning so much and you talk about your cool teacher at home and all the parents get so excited they look like they're going to pass out. Then you repeat what the teacher said about evolution or gays in front of the right kid's parents, like those Anglos who have those little blue and white signs with the Ten Commandments sticking up in their front yard, and—boom!—that teacher is history.

We didn't even have to pretend we liked Beecher to get her to say stuff she could get fired for. Like when Joey Dinwiddie said he and his girl were going to get married, Beecher said, "I bet you think if you get married, you'll be able to have sex every day." Joey laid back in his chair and puffed up his chest. "Damn right," he said with his big talking-about-pussy grin.

"I hate to disappoint you," Beecher said, "but getting married is the best way to make sure you don't have sex every day. If you don't believe me, go home and ask your father."

Everybody started making kissing noises and shouting out stuff about sex and a bunch of kids stood up and did some air-humping. Beecher held up her hands and said, "You children obviously are not mature enough to be sexually active. If your only goal when you have sex is to experience an orgasm, then you are masturbating on other people. You would do better to have sex with yourself. No danger of disease, no possible pregnancy—and no broken hearts."

Kids started screaming their heads off as soon as Beecher said masturbate. Beecher didn't even blush. She just waited until the screaming died down. Then she said, "My point exactly. If you cannot say the words *penis, vagina, breast, orgasm,* and *masturbation* without giggling and blushing, then you are not mature enough to have sex."

Somebody ratted out Beecher for telling us to masturbate.

Teeny White who works as a student clerk in the office said she saw Beecher go into Mrs. Nichols's office and Teeny could hear Nichols hollering and when Beecher came out it looked like she was crying. But there's so many pregnant girls in our school that they can't fire anybody for talking about sex because then it would get in the papers and the parents in this town freak out totally if they even see the words *sex* and *school* on the same page.

Mrs. Nichols visited our class the next day and sat in the back and wrote a bunch of notes and we figured Beecher was history but nothing happened. We couldn't figure it. Beecher isn't local, so she couldn't have cousins on the school board and nobody in her family is a county commissioner. Usually it only takes a month to get rid of a new teacher. Two minutes is our all-time record. But if they make it to the end of first quarter, they usually last a whole year. Beecher was still going strong by Halloween and we started to think she might make it, but then she read us this story the day before Halloween. It was just one of those dumb ghost stories that are supposed to be spooky and scary but only little kids are scared of them. Beecher lit candles and turned out the lights and put on some weird, spaced-out music. It was actually pretty interesting and everybody was kind of getting into it, but about halfway through the story, Beecher read the word *damn* or *hell* or something like that. Nothing, really. Not even a real swearword. But this is Rosablanca, so when we came back to school the next day, T.J. Ritchie's mom ran screaming into the principal's office and said Beecher was preaching Satanism and T.J. had been traumatized by the experience.

I heard it all because me and Jaime Sanchez were outside the main entrance trying to jack the change out of the pay phone. I seen Beecher going into Mrs. Nichols's office and then the bell rang and we went to class and everybody was psyched because we didn't have a teacher. Then this counselor showed up and took roll and started talking about how much more money we'd make in our life if we graduated from high school instead of dropping out. I wondered what that counselor would say if I told him that T.J. Ritchie already makes a lot more money than he does and T.J. don't pay no taxes on it, neither.

Beecher showed up about ten minutes before the bell rang, but she didn't say anything, just collected all her stuff. Her eyes were all red from crying. The counselor smiled real cheesy at Beecher and ducked out and we just sat there so quiet I could hear the clock above the door that only has a minute hand and stutters just like Jerome Harding. T-tick t-tick t-tick. The ticking made me think about when Beecher said the most important thing she could teach us was to choose how to spend our time because your time is your life.

After Beecher had gathered up her stuff and walked over to the door, she turned around and opened her mouth partways like she was going to say something. I thought maybe she was going to say it was no big deal and she would see us in the morning, but she didn't. She just hooked her hair

11

behind her ears with her fingers and looked at us all, one kid at a time. I thought she might skip over T.J. Ritchie, but she didn't. She looked at him exactly as long as she looked at me and her face didn't change. I thought she would of changed her face a little bit when she looked at me.

Nobody said anything, not even the kiss-ass girls. I almost said something. I almost said, *"Hasta luego,"* but I didn't because one little thing like that is enough to make a teacher think you care whether they live or die. If they think you give one little shit about them, they start working on you, trying to wear you down. Tell me your story, they say, I want to help you but I can't help you if you don't let me. Just tell me the truth. They think they want to know the truth. They think they can handle it. But they can't even handle the easy shit like how come Joey Dinwiddie's brother got straight A's and a full ride to some college out in Oklahoma where they promised him he'd be the starting quarterback but he sat on the bench for two years with the only other black kid on the team and watched dumb white farmers fumble every play until he got disgusted and came home. He didn't waste his education or anything. He got a job coaching at the regular high school, but if a really smart kid like Dinwiddie couldn't make it, then what kind of chance is there for us regular everyday losers. None of the teachers ever has a good answer to the Dinwiddie question because there isn't one. That's just the way it is. Beecher might of thought of something, but by the time she showed up, Joey was tired of telling that story and the rest of us were tired of hearing it.

Every once in a while, when a teacher is too dense to get the message that they're not really here to teach, they're just here to fill in the roll sheets so the alt school won't lose its funding and the regular school won't have to deal with us, Denny Clodfelter pretends like he's real interested in reading the stupid stories in our literature book. He even volunteers to read out loud, which just about makes the English teacher pee her pants. Then, after the teacher gets all excited about finding a punk who appreciates literature, Denny will stop reading one day right in the middle of some story and he'll say, "You know, after your dad breaks a two-by-four across your face and you have to go around for the rest of your life looking like a flat-faced heifer, you just can't care about reading these stories. Like you can't get excited about some idiot who sells his fancy watch to buy some hair combs for his wife except she sold her hair to buy him a chain for his watch. Besides, that whole story is just bogus because who would want to buy some old used hair anyway."

I bet somebody would buy Beecher's hair, though, even if it was used because it's so shiny like it has a million candles lit inside it. When she was standing in the doorway, trying to feel some kind of goodbye from us, I thought about giving her my journal that I never turned in after she asked us to write one important thing from our life. I wrote like six pages about how it feels to be a eight-year-old kid who idolizes his older cousin so much and how exciting it was when he finally let me ride with him one night and what a thrill it was to drink a cold *cerveza* and smoke a Marlboro with my arm leaning out

13

the window of that car with the killer speakers and chrome spinners. And how it felt to watch my cousin get out of the car and leave the engine running and walk up and knock on this kid's door and then blow the kid's face off the second he opened the door and how I shit my pants and sat in it all the way home, smelling the stink of hopelessness that hung around my life.

I didn't give Beecher my journal, though. I figured she already had enough stuff to make her feel bad. Now she'll probably go teach some Indian kids on a reservation in Arizona like she used to talk about sometimes. It'll probably be easier out there. I don't think they have so much gangs and stuff because they got tribes and drums and sweat lodges. We learned about all that during Native American Heritage Week. Beecher brought in all these Indian stories but she knew we never read our homework so she read us this one story out loud. It was written by this guy named Alexie who is a real Indian, and it was a pretty long story but it wasn't even boring. It was pretty sad, though, and I know Beecher read it to us because then we would see that our life isn't so bad because at least we got indoor plumbing and floors instead of just dirt and the government doesn't try to take away our language anymore.

Maybe those Indian kids will appreciate Beecher. Maybe they'll like having a teacher that calls up their parents and comes to their house to shake their hands and sit on their falling-apart furniture to show how much she cares. Maybe

14

those kids won't break the windows in her car while she's inside their house. They might even like her after a while. But
we don't like that kind of teacher here. We don't need people feeling sorry for us. We need those hard teachers, the ones
who know what it feels like to wake up hungry every day for
sixteen years. The ones who catch you all by yourself in the
hallway and grab your shirt and slam you up against the wall
and say, "You're such a fucking loser," and then just drop their
hands and shake their heads and walk away. Those kinds of
teachers might be able to handle the truth if I ever felt like
telling them, but I doubt if I ever will. What difference would
it make if I did?

CHAPTER 3

BACK WHERE YOU CAME FROM

TODAY IN SCHOOL THIS NEW KID FROM OHIO SAID PEOPLE IN New Mexico are lazy because everybody on his street parks their car right up in their yard near the front door where you would have some nice grass if you lived in one of those green places.

"I don't see why they can't even walk a couple steps to their door," the stupid Ohio kid said, and I was going to explain that his neighbors might be lazy but probably that isn't why they park in their yard because if they don't got a handicap ramp and they park right in front of their door then they could be a dealer or some kind of gangster who doesn't want to get shot trying to get from his house to his car or vice versa. But I didn't tell him because Henry Dominguez already told

16

him to shut up and go back where he came from if he didn't like it here. The Ohio kid's ears got all red and I felt kind of sorry for him because I don't know how many times somebody told me to go back where I came from except I am where I came from and they're too stupid to know it—even though everybody has to take American history and it's right there in the book that a whole bunch of states used to be Mexico, like Texas and New Mexico and Arizona. Like *mi abuelo* always says, "We didn't cross the border, *mijo*. The border crossed us. The Corazons been living here for three hundred years."

When Beecher was here, we used to have some pretty good class discussions about stuff because Beecher was like one of those little sheepdogs that you see on the Discovery Channel where they don't make any noise, but they keep all the sheeps going in the right direction and if one of the sheeps starts getting any big ideas and gets out of line, the little dog just bites it on the butt. But our new *pinche* dickhead teacher Mr. McElroy believes in democracy and it doesn't work any better in our English class than it does in our government because only the real big guys get free speech and everybody else knows if they say what they really think who's going to be waiting to whack them after class. McElroy tried to start a discussion about the border controversy after Henry told the Ohio kid to go back where he came from and the Ohio kid told Henry to go back where he came from, but as soon as McElroy asked for comments, T.J. Ritchie laid back in his chair and said why don't we let those Minutemen who

17

bring all their guns and sit on the border in their lawn chairs just get up off their asses and do what everybody knows they want to do.

"If we just let those Border Patrol wannabes shoot the stupid Mexicans, then we wouldn't have a border problem," T.J. said. He doesn't give a shit about the border, but he likes to get things started.

"That would be murder, you stupid ass," said Teeny White, whose mother is Mexican.

"Those Minutemen guys are the ones who are stupid," T.J. said. "I mean, I'm white and everything—"

"You sure about that?" Henry Dominguez hollered, and the tortilla crowd cheered. But T.J. Ritchie doesn't care if you say shit about him being white because he's always saying there are two kinds of white people and he thinks he's one of the good kind because his mother drags him to church all the time and he knows a whole bunch of quotations from the Bible. They're mostly quotations about why it's okay to hate other people like gays or Arabs, but if anybody reminds T.J. that Jesus didn't hate people, he just says, "Oh yeah? I'll pray for you to stop being so stupid next time I go to church."

"Those Minutemen are mostly those big fat dumb white boys who like to drive around the desert chasing down antelope and shooting them from inside their pickups," T.J. said. "They call that hunting. Effing assholes."

Then a bunch of other white boys who cut school every year during hunting season said maybe they should have open season on idiots like T.J., and McElroy blew his whistle and gave us a spelling quiz. I kind of wished McElroy knew how to have a discussion because I had an idea when everybody was yelling. I was thinking what would happen if Canada decided they wanted to have more land, just like America did back when they invaded Mexico. I looked it up on the Internet. In our history book, it says "the Mexican-American War," but in the Mexico history books it says "the United States Invasion of Mexico." Anyway, so the Canadians just decide to take Wisconsin and Minnesota and some of those other cold states up there where all the lakes are. And they have to kick some butt and kill a bunch of people, but they win and then they put up this big fence and say, "Now this is Canada and you can't come here and live unless we say so." And some people would say, "But our family has lived here for three generations." Or they would say, "My grandmother lives over there and I always visit her on weekends." But Canada would say, "Tough shit. Handle it. And you can't come here and work anymore, either, unless we say so. Even if you already worked here for years." And Americans would say, "How come you're acting so shitty instead of trying to get along with your neighbors?" But Canada wouldn't have to answer that question because they already got what they wanted. And Americans would just keep on sneaking over the border because they would feel like nobody has the right to split up families or just take somebody's land and say it's another country and then Canada would get real pissed and say,

"Okay, we're making French the official language. How do you like them *manzanas?*" But probably if you tried to ask some Americans to think about my Canadian idea they would just look at you weird and tell you to go back where you came from.

Anyway, all I'm saying is you should drive around the neighborhood at night and see if there are any cars parked in the yard right up by the front door before you buy a house in New Mexico, but if some new family is too stupid to figure that out then they'll just end up freaking out and moving anyway, so it works out the same in the end.

CHAPTER 4

JUST SAY NO

PEOPLE SHOULDN'T BE ALLOWED TO GO AROUND TELLING LIT-
tle kids to Just Say No to drugs because that could be dangerous. Besides, Just Say No has to be one of the lamest ideas
ever invented in the first place and I bet it was invented by
somebody white who never had to sleep in the same bed with
four other people who hardly don't ever take a shower because there wasn't anyplace else to sleep. If just saying no
worked then people would go around just saying no to stuff
they didn't want to do anymore. Papi could just say no to being poor and unemployed. People would just say no to cigarettes and they wouldn't have to pay all that money to get
hypnotized into quitting smoking. And all those white girls
wouldn't be puking up French fries in the bathroom behind

21

the cafeteria. And Bobby Chavez wouldn't be dead. Bobby said no. Except he said no to the wrong guys and they popped him just like that. And then they put it in the paper that it was a drug deal gone bad, all insinuating that Bobby was buying drugs, which was the first thing that came to most people's mind anyway because he was poor and brown.

It didn't matter that Bobby was president of the Spanish Club and the best player on the soccer team and made the honor roll every single time. They forgot all that stuff as soon as the newspapers said there were drugs involved when the incident went down. The teachers all made little speeches about how much everybody would miss Bobby, but you could see it in their eyes that they believed all those lies in the paper and what they really wanted to say was, "See what happens to you when you waste your potential and take drugs?" And even though a bunch of kids tried to tell them that Bobby wasn't buying, nobody paid any attention to them. The police and the newspapers and the television reporters all commentated and speculated that Bobby got caught buying a little recreational cocaine and *tsk tsk tsk* what a shame because he had so much potential. Even that Latina reporter from the TV station down in El Paso sat there in her sharp suit with her hair that doesn't move and pretended·like she knew what she was talking about.

That's when I stopped reading newspapers and watching the TV news because those guys are supposed to be investigative reporters but even an idiot like T.J. Ritchie could have made a better investigation than they did. All they would have had to do was go to my neighborhood and stand on the corner and watch. And they'd see that black pickup with the black-tinted windows sitting right behind the bus stop. They'd see the bus pull up and all the kids start piling out the door and when the last couple of kids got off the bus, the door of that pickup would open and a real big guy in a black sweat suit with a black watch cap would get out and start walking behind those last kids. And the kids would walk a little bit faster and the blood in their ears would pound like that sound track from *Jaws* when the shark is circling the boat, getting ready to chomp their arms and legs off. And they'd see this one kid who was walking alone, like I made the mistake of doing a couple weeks after Bobby got popped. Then they'd see that big guy in the sweat suit grab that all-alone kid and put a gun up to his head and say, "Here's the package. Here's the address. Here's the money. Deliver it or you're dead." And the kid would deliver the package because he wasn't stupid enough to Just Say No. And the next day, that kid would get the message that if he didn't show up on the corner and do another delivery, the cops would be knocking on his door to bust him for dealing drugs and they wouldn't believe him if he told them about the black pickup and the gun because he's a poor Mexican kid from a bad neighborhood, so the cops figure he's theirs sooner or later and it might as well be sooner. And the kid would know that black truck would be waiting by the bus stop the next day, and he couldn't say no to drugs, so that kid and his cousins would make a gang and he would never have to walk alone again.

CHAPTER 5

ME AND HARVEY CASTRO

Okay, here's the difference between me and Harvey Castro who lives next door to me except it's like we live on different planets. Harvey's friendly and everything but we don't hang together because he's a senior at the regular school and I'm only a junior at the alt school. Plus, Harvey is from Nicaragua which doesn't really matter except all the Anglo teachers think he's Mexican because he has black hair and speaks Spanish. Most Anglos are like that but it isn't their fault because they don't get a very good education about us. In elementary school they probably learn the Mexican hat dance and color in the geography maps for South America and Central America and memorize where the coffee beans come from, but by the time they get to high school they don't

24

know the difference between El Salvador and Ecuador. They read about two pages in the history books and then they forget all about south of the border except for the tequila and the drugs and the mariachi dancers and the coffee. This one time, Beecher told us she bought this special fair-trade coffee that was picked by people in Ecuador who didn't get ripped off by the big coffee companies. But I bet those people were still real poor because if they weren't, why would they spend all day picking coffee beans for rich Americans who spend so much money on one cup of coffee that they could have bought five breakfast burritos instead?

Anyway, Harvey is from Nicaragua so when he came here they put him in ESL class because he had a real big accent and nobody could understand him for about a year and after that they realized he was some kind of genius so they switched him to Advanced Placement where he has been kicking Anglo ass ever since.

Harvey is short and round and everybody calls him Gordito but he has a mustache and a girlfriend who has been engaged to him for two whole years. I'm tall and skinny and I have about three hairs on my chin and the longest I ever had a girlfriend was for one week. I met Angela when I was working as a bagger at Kmart over at White Sands Mall and she worked at Chick-fil-A. I probably wouldn't have even met her except we got off work at the same time and we both liked that bourbon chicken from the Chinese takeout. The first couple times I saw her, I didn't say anything because she was too pretty to talk to. But the third time I saw her, she brought her bourbon chicken over and sat down at the same little table where I was sitting and said, "Hi, I'm Angela," and after that she was my girlfriend.

A couple days later, we were walking around the mall after work and Angela said she was cold, so I bought her a leather jacket. The next day, she said she didn't want to miss my calls, so I bought her a cell phone. Then I didn't see her at work for a couple days, so my cousin Graciela who is in the same class with Angela drove me over to Tularosa where Angela lives. When I knocked on the door, this big buff *güero* answered the door and told me to get lost and leave his girlfriend alone or he would mess me up good. I said what about all the stuff I bought her and he said, "That's your loss, sucker." He poked his finger in my chest, too, right in front of *mi prima*. I got so mad I drove like a maniac all the way home and I drove into a irrigation ditch and hit a little tree and broke it. Graciela had to go to the hospital but she was all right and she didn't sue me or anything because she's family and she felt sorry for me because it took me about six months to pay for that stupid tree. And now I have to walk or skateboard everyplace because Papi took my car away and gave me a bicycle which I wouldn't ride if you paid me because then everybody would see that I'm a loser.

Harvey Castro rides a bike. He rides it every single day, even when it rains, but he never looks sweaty and his hair doesn't move. He has this kind of long hair that he combs straight back from his forehead and it never moves. I think it looks wack like those old TV game show guys but all the girls think Harvey is cute. That's what they always say. "Ooh, Harvey is so cute." And if the guys make fun of Harvey for being cute, he just laughs and says, "Do you want my autograph now while you can still afford it?"

No matter what anybody says to Harvey, he won't fight. He's too smart to fight. In fact, he was going to be the valedictorian of his class when he graduates. I don't even know if I'm going to graduate or not. It depends. But Harvey already has a scholarship to go to the University of New Mexico. He got invited to go to a bunch of other colleges, even some rich ones like Harvard, but he says he doesn't want to go too far away in case his parents need him for something.

Harvey should be the valedictorian because he has a 5.0 GPA on account of all his extra credits for taking college classes and being president of the student council and all kinds of community service stuff that he didn't even have to do. The only time I ever did community service was when I got caught shoplifting. But last week, the principal at Rosablanca High called Harvey's parents and told them that they should be so proud of their son for being number two. Now he's the studitorian or some lame title like that. Even though everybody knows Harvey is *número uno* and he has the highest GPA, it doesn't count because he was in ESL for a year and ESL credits don't count the same as regular classes. So they took away being the valedictorian. Harvey's mother called up my mother and told her all about it and I thought, *Híjole! Watch out!* because now Harvey is going to let them have it—but the next day he just walked around the neighborhood like normal. He didn't even act like he was pissed.

Henry Dominguez asked Harvey was he going to sue the school and Harvey just laughed and said, "It's just high school. It doesn't really matter."

That's the real difference between Harvey and me. Things don't matter to him like they do to me. I would of burned down the school or at least tore a toilet off the wall in the bathroom. But that's why I'm in the alt school and Harvey Castro isn't even though I used to get straight A's before I started being a juvenile delinquent. Harvey's parents are poor just like mine, and he's the oldest kid just like me, and he's Catholic and his father kicks his ass just like Papi does mine, so how come Harvey's so cool and I'm so hot? How come he just walks away from fights and does his homework and gets a college scholarship and I flunk biology and attract fights like mosquitoes on a summer night? Is it in my genes? Or did my parents do something wrong? Or am I just who I am by accident?

I used to think I was messed up because of being a sex offender in the second grade. I wasn't really a sex offender but that's what the school labeled me after I kicked my teacher in the crotch. I didn't mean to kick her in the crotch, neither. I was just trying to get her to let go of my ear. She was this real mean little teacher who used to twist the boys' ears all the time, anytime we did even the littlest thing wrong, and sometimes when we didn't even do nothing. She would just grab your ear and twist it until it felt like she was ripping it right off your head and we would all cry, even T.J. Ritchie, because it hurt real bad. And this one day, I had a ear infection and I even had a note from my mother saying I shouldn't have to take gym class and that teacher knew I had a ear infection but she twisted my ear anyway. I yelled at her to stop but she wouldn't. And I tried to hit her but my arms were too short. She just held her arm out straight and practically picked me up off the floor by my ear. So I kicked her. I wasn't aiming at any special place. I just kicked and my foot went right between her legs.

It was a total accident. I didn't even know where I kicked her. I was just glad she finally let go of my ear. But the next thing you know, they had the security guards and the police and the psychologist and the nurse and everybody all interrogating me and asking me questions. I can't even remember what they asked me because my ear hurt so much that mostly I just nodded my head because I didn't want to say anything because then I would start crying like a little baby in front of all those people.

They put me out of school for a week and when I came back all the kids acted like I was Rambo or something. T.J. Ritchie said I was a real badass and I thought that was so cool, so I pretended like I meant to kick that teacher. And I said I would kick her again if she came near me, so they put me in another teacher's room and I could tell right away that she was afraid of me and I thought, How cool is that, a teacher being afraid of you when you're only seven years old. So every time she looked at me, I messed up my face and tried to look like a real mean badass.

After that, they started sending me to talk to this lady in a suit every Friday when we were supposed to have recess and she asked me to draw pictures and play with toys and make up stories about all kinds of weird things, like what would I do if I had a little baby and I was the father and would I punch that baby if it cried. I liked that lady because she had a nice soft voice and she never yelled or twisted my ears. At the end of second grade, I never saw that lady again but when I went to third grade, they put me in special ed. Not the special ed for dumb kids but the special ed for kids who don't know how to act. I told them I already knew how to act but nobody listened to me, so I showed them I could act like those idiots. I drew pictures of *chichis* on my desk and threw gummy bears up so they stuck on the lights, and sneezed *mocos* all over the hair of the girl who sat in front of me—then they started making me take those pills. I took them for a couple of months but they made me feel spastic, so I started throwing them away until T.J. Ritchie told me I could sell them.

It really wasn't such a big deal. I could have kept on telling those people what happened until somebody believed me. Or I could have just said I was sorry for kicking that teacher and started getting A's again, but I was too stubborn and so mad. Even way back then when I was little, I was mad about how they treat boys different. When girls do mean things, people always think they were abused or something. When a boy does something mean, even by accident, people usually think he's a future felon, especially if the boy is Mexican.

Still, I could have brushed it all off just like Harvey Castro brushed off getting his valedictorian award stolen by the school. But I can't brush off nothing. Not even little stuff. Everything just sticks to me. And all those little things just weigh me down so much that I feel like my bones are made of stone and if I walked into the Rio Grande I would sink to the bottom so fast that I wouldn't even make a ripple and nobody would even notice I was gone.

CHAPTER 6

WALKING WITH A COP

T.J. Ritchie is a no-brain stoner, but you got to give him props for having big *cojones*. T.J. just says what he thinks no matter what. Part of the reason is because he's so big, I think, but the other part is because he really believes he has everything figured out. Like yesterday, when we were discussing current events in McElroy's class, and this one black kid said what about that black guy who didn't do nothing and didn't even have a gun and he got killed by the cops right before he was supposed to get married and why does that shit keep happening, T.J. said, "Because *you* people let it happen, dipshit."

Everybody started hollering different stuff at T.J. and the black kid looked around real fast, like he was looking for his homies to back him up, except if you're black in Rosablanca, you're on your own. We only got like six black kids in the whole school. McElroy banged his ruler on his desk, which is the signal for everybody to stop talking, but T.J. kept right on going.

"I'm serious," T.J. said. "The cops don't do nothing about it and the government sure ain't gonna do nothing about it, so the regular good black people need to do something about it. Whenever a cop kills a innocent black guy who wasn't even strapped, then some other regular black people need to kill that cop. If the cop kills two black guys, they need to kill that cop and his partner so they'll know how it feels to get killed just for being who you are. If they can't get to the cop, they should kill his wife or one of his kids. And don't just shoot them once, neither. They got to shoot them forty or fifty times, because that's what the cops do to those guys. You know the guy is dead after the first or second shot, but they keep on shooting and shooting so the guy can't get better and sue them. Bang bang bang bang bang bang bang bang bang bang. Dead dead dead dead dead dead dead dead dead dead dead—"

"Shut up!" Teeny White covered her ears. "You're crazy. You're making me sick." And a bunch of other kids started yelling at T.J. to shut up because he was advocating hate crimes. McElroy tried to act like he was in charge of everything. He huffed up to his desk and wrote T.J. a referral to the office, but T.J. just crumpled up the referral and threw it on the floor. He stood up and kicked the back of his chair so hard that one of the bolts came loose and the chair sort of flopped sideways like T.J. had killed it, too.

"I ain't advocating nothing," T.J. said. "I'm just saying if you want people to understand how something feels, sometimes you have to do the same thing to them. Like if we could lock all the teachers in one big room and treat them like shit, maybe some of them would stop acting like such fucking jerks to us." He glared at McElroy who ran over to the red phone and called security. T.J. just laughed and shook his head and pointed at McElroy. "See what I'm talking about? Can't even have an honest discussion about anything. If you don't say what they want, or if you treat them like they treat you, they beat you down or lock you up."

T.J. walked over to the doorway and slammed himself up against the wall and held his arms out in front with his wrists together like he was waiting to get handcuffed. When security showed up it was just the little blond lady guard. She looks like a kid but up close you can tell she's old enough to be your mother. They always send her to get T.J. because they probably think he wouldn't beat up a female, especially a old one. He would if he wanted to, though. I know he would, except then he would go to real jail instead of just juvi where he has a lot of friends so he doesn't care. He won't even get sent to juvi for killing a chair and being disruptive, though. He'll just get a three-day vacation which is supposed to give him time to think about his behavior and realize he needs to learn some anger-management skills, but he'll just sit at home and drink his dad's beer and smoke some dope and play video games and watch some porn if he can find his dad's new hiding place.

When the security lady walked in, T.J. slammed himself up against the wall again and held out his wrists, but the lady just laughed and pointed to the door. T.J. took a couple steps and then turned back around and said, "You guys should think about what I said. If I was a black guy and I said all that shit, you know they would lock me up like they did Huey Newton or kill me like they did Malcolm X. But I'm white and I don't even like black people that much."

T.J. shot a look at the black kid and shoved his hands into his pockets. "Sorry, but that's just how I am. I say what a lot of people are probably thinking and everybody can pretend they didn't think it and call me crazy and stupid. And maybe my idea is crazy, but it ain't stupid. I'm not stupid."

"That's enough," McElroy told us after T.J. finally followed the security lady outside, but nobody was talking. We were all trying not to look at the black kid. And I could tell that some of the other kids were thinking about T.J.'s idea too. I mean, I don't think killing people is such a great idea, especially cops, because then your life is really over. Plus, even cops who are prejudiced probably have kids or a wife or a mother who loves them even if they're a stupid jerk. But in a way T.J. was right. Teachers ask us to have a discussion but then if they don't like what we say, they tell us to shut up.

And he's right about making people think, too. Sometimes you got to knock people down and shove the other guy's shoes onto their feet before they will walk a mile in them.

T.J. looked different walking beside that little security guard. He didn't look small, because he's too big to look small, but even from the back, you could tell he knew everybody was watching him get walked by security. Like he was walking beside his grandmother or like he was walking beside a real cop.

You walk different when you walk beside a cop because it's like you can see yourself and you think, Do I look like a rat who just turned on his homies to save his ass? Or, Do I look like a pervert who just passed by the elementary school with his pants unzipped and his dog hanging out? I hope I don't look like somebody stupid enough to sell meth because that shit is death, man. I'm pretty sure I don't look like a cop, even a undercover cop, because cops have a look in their eyes like if you mess up I will rip your liver out and eat it for lunch. I don't think that's what my eyes say, even when I try to look all kick-ass. The worst my eyes probably say is maybe I'm not that good of a fighter but I go down hard.

I walked with a cop once, right here at Bright Horizons. I wasn't getting arrested or anything. I was being an escort. Beecher wrote to the police and asked them did they want to come over and give a pep talk to her class so we might decide to stop being juvenile delinquents. We didn't think the cops would come—Hey, that reminds me of this baseball cap *mi primo* Enrique used to wear all the time that says CALL 911. MAKE A COP COME. Primo had to stop wearing it because the cops didn't think it was too funny—anyways, we didn't think the cops would waste their time talking to us, especially since most of us already did too much talking to the cops out on the street, but Beecher got a letter from this one cop, Sergeant Chris Cabrera, who said he would be honored to be our guest speaker.

Beecher picked me to escort Sgt. Cabrera from the office to our room because I made the mistake of telling T.J. Ritchie to shut up after he said, "Oh goody. I'm going to take notes when he's talking so I can learn how to be a better person." I told T.J. to get a little respect because Cabrera could have just flipped us off and Beecher said, "Eddie is absolutely right." And then she asked me to stay after class so she could explain my escort duties.

"Hey, you're a male escort," Henry Dominguez said.

"Men don't call male escorts, you idiot," T.J. said, and Teeny White said, "Uh-huh. Some of them do," but Beecher cut that discussion off at the neck because she could see where it was headed. And when Sgt. Cabrera showed up and the office called me to come and get him, he turned out to be a she. It used to be all the cops were men but now they got girl cops in all kinds of sizes and even the little ones can kick your butt pretty good with their bare hands.

Sgt. Cabrera wasn't little. She was taller than me, probably five-ten, and she looked like she might do a little weight training on the side because she had her sleeves rolled up and her biceps were pretty cut and you could see the veins bulging on her wrists just like the bodybuilders. She told me she was from Puerto Rico but everybody thinks she's Mexican because she lives in New Mexico, even the Mexicans. I told her they should know better because she doesn't sound Mexican to me, she sounds like New York and she said, "Bingo!" and aimed her hand at me like a gun and shot me, except she was smiling, so I shot her back.

"What are you going to do after you graduate?" she asked me right before we got to Beecher's room. I told her I wasn't sure I would graduate because of various things and she said, "You mean you haven't decided to make it happen?" and she nodded like she knew everything about me. I was glad we got to the room right after that because even though she was friendly and everything, it made me feel nervous when she looked me in the eye. She didn't have the rip-your-liver-out look. She had a nice look, kind of like Beecher, except Sgt. Cabrera's look had some kind of extra power, like X-ray vision or something and you could tell she could cut right through whatever shit you tried to throw at her. All during her talk, I felt like she was staring at me even though she probably wasn't. I stayed in my seat when everybody was clapping after she finished inspiring us, hoping that Beecher would just let Sgt. Cabrera walk back to the office herself since she knew where it was, but both of them stood there and smiled at me, so I had to be her escort again.

I thought Sgt. Cabrera would give me a lecture or maybe ask me a bunch of questions on the way to the office, but she didn't. She just asked me did I like to read and I said yes only please don't tell anybody because I got a reputation to maintain, and she said I should read *The Four Agreements* by this guy named Don Miguel Ruiz.

"It's a real short book," she said, "and it sounds too simple, but if you really think about what it says, you realize it's very deep and it can change your life."

I nodded but I didn't say what I was thinking was that my life could use some change but not the kind you get from reading a little book. My life would need an encyclopedia.

"It might even make you decide to graduate, muchacho." Sgt. Cabrera winked at me like we had some big secret going and I was glad there was nobody else around.

"It's not up to me," I said. "I don't have enough credits and I'm flunking biology."

"You're only a junior," Sgt. Cabrera said. "You have a whole summer and another year ahead of you. Why not think positive? Your thoughts create your intentions and your intentions create your reality." She winked at me again. "That's from the book."

"Yeah, thanks," I said, and then I walked faster so I could get that crazy cop to the office and get rid of her. She must of gone to high school or they wouldn't let her join the police but she must of forgot what it's like. If you want to graduate high school, you have to be a liar. You have to pretend you care about stuff you don't care about, like what does a frog's guts look like and how to multiply fractions, and you have to keep your mouth shut when you feel like talking but then you have to talk when you don't feel like it, except you have to say what you're supposed to say and not what you really think. You have to wear clothes you don't like and act respectful to people who need a good punch in the face.

Papi is always telling me to just act like I respect everybody and life will be easier. Like he always tells me to just shut up and do what the teachers tell me and I won't have any more troubles. And I know he tells me to keep my big fat *boca* shut because he can't do it, neither, which is why he doesn't have a job right now. He always gets hired on construction crews when they first start up because he's big and fast. He can swing a hammer with both hands so good that he only needs one hit per nail and if they put him on one end of a two-by-twelve and a guy with a nail gun on the other end, they end up meeting in the middle. But if the boss talks down to him or says one thing about wetbacks or beaners or sometimes if they even just ask if anybody wants Taco Bell for lunch, Papi just flips the guy off and picks up his lunch pail and heads for his truck. And the next time that foreman needs a crew, Papi doesn't even try to get on because he would have to say he was sorry when he wasn't.

If it wasn't for my mother, I wouldn't even stay in school for one second, but I promised her I would graduate and set a good example for Letty and Juanito and my little cousins. I didn't promise her on purpose, but I promised her and she never forgets that kind of stuff, especially since I don't hardly hang around with her too much anymore. We used to sit in the living room and read sometimes after supper and sometimes even on the weekend if I didn't have something better to do, but now I rather read by myself. Not that I don't like my mother—I even love her—but after you get to be like ten years old it's too weird to sit around with your mother.

That's what I was doing when I accidentally promised to graduate. Sitting there reading. Letty was reading, too, and even Juanito was being quiet for a change, but I couldn't concentrate because Mami kept sighing and blowing her nose in a tissue. I asked her was she sick and she just sighed again and didn't answer me. She's usually the smiling one in our house, so I started thinking what could be wrong with her if she wasn't sick and Papi wasn't even there to make her cry.

As soon as I thought of Papi, I remembered that he told me a couple of weeks earlier don't forget Mami's birthday. But I forgot and I figured he did, too, because it was almost seven o'clock and he wasn't even home yet. I didn't have any money to go out and get something, so I went in my room and looked around to see if there was any kind of good junk that I could give Mami for a present. But there wasn't anything. So I took a piece of paper and drew a swirly border all around the edges and wrote OFFICIAL CERTIFICATE in big letters at the top. Then I filled it in like one of those gift certificates the *viejas* give you at Christmas so you can spend $20 at some store, or $50 once in a while if the *vieja* is rich, except instead of money, I wrote it out real fancy that I promised to stay in school and graduate. I signed it with my official signature and printed my whole name underneath.

Mami started crying for real when I gave her that certificate and I felt pretty good for about two minutes until we heard a big noise out in the backyard and we looked out the window and there was Papi standing beside this little crape myrtle tree with pink flowers all over it. Mami ran outside and started jumping up and down because she kept wanting one of those trees but you can't hardly find them in Rosablanca. And there was a little white box hanging on the tree with a pink ribbon around it. Mami handed Papi my certificate and grabbed the box and opened it and there was some diamond earrings inside. While she was putting on the earrings, Papi read my certificate, but he didn't say anything, just looked at me hard for a couple seconds and then folded the certificate up and gave it back to Mami.

We had homemade *sopapillas* for dessert that night with lots of honey because Mami was happy about so many things. Not just the earrings and the crape myrtle tree and my certificate. I knew she was the happiest because she knew Papi really was working overtime the last couple months like he said and not doing something he shouldn't be doing, which is what she had been thinking. She never said it, but I could tell by the way her mouth got real tight whenever she looked at the clock in the kitchen while she was fixing supper and the way she watched Papi eat when he wasn't looking.

If I would have waited a couple minutes longer that day, we would have heard Papi before I went and made that dumb certificate. Mami hung it on the refrigerator, so I have to see it every time I want some juice or an apple or something. I thought about hiding it or tearing it up, but it wouldn't get me out of the deal because I already put it in writing and everybody in the family read it a hundred times. It's probably a good thing I wrote it down, though, because otherwise I might have dropped out of school one of those days when I felt like breaking all the windows just to make something interesting happen instead of all those dumb assignments and tests.

Being a good example is hard work but at least it makes me feel like I'm doing something and not just taking up space. I'd like to take up a real big space someday, so big that people would have to stand back when I walk into the room, but I would act like I didn't even notice they were looking at me. That way, people wouldn't feel embarrassed and they could take a good long look at me and maybe they would see something in me that is so good I can't even see it myself.

CHAPTER 7

I GOT A GIRLFRIEND

Yo, I finally got a girlfriend. A real one, too, not the kind you have to pay just so you can touch her. And I didn't even have to use any of the pickup lines Primo made me practice for two weeks after Angela turned out not to be my girlfriend.

"You got to act like you notice a woman," Enrique said, "and you got to let her know you think she's fine, but not so fine that she could have you just like that." He snapped his fingers and stuck his chin up in the air. He thinks that makes him look like a *chingón* movie star but it really makes him look just like that little bobblehead Chihuahua he glued to the dashboard of his Camaro.

Anyway, I didn't have to say anything cool or walk like a

44

panther or flash my new cell phone or anything. All I did was sign up for ballroom dance. I could have signed up last semester when Beecher tried to get a bunch of us guys to sign up, but back then I thought ballroom dancing was too gay for a guy like me.

"You can get the fine arts credits you need to graduate and you'll meet lots of girls," Beecher told us. "And let me tell you, girls love to dance. They don't care if you don't dance very well. They will like you just for trying." But we still wouldn't do it. At first, T.J. Ritchie said he was going to, so some other guys said they would, too, but then T.J. snorted and spit a big wet one into the trash can and said, "You pussies have a good time," so nobody signed up.

This semester, I decided to give it a try after I watched one of those dance shows because I was thinking, Yo, look at those dudes—they're touching those girls. And all the girls on that show looked so fine. I didn't think the girls at Bright Horizons would be as fine as the girls on television, but at least they would be real live girls and I would get to look at them up close and hold their hands while we were dancing.

There was only three guys in the whole class and twenty-three girls. At first, I was thinking I would just ask for a bathroom pass and never come back, but the teacher was standing way on the other side of the gym and I didn't want to walk across that whole floor and ask to go to the bathroom with all those girls watching me because you know how girls are. They were standing real close to each other and giggling and grabbing each other and pretending they were interested in what each other was saying when all the time what they were really doing was checking out the dudes. All except this one girl who was sort of standing off to the side by herself. Not like she was stuck-up or shy. Just like she was the kind of girl who could stand alone and not care about it.

I was so busy looking at the girls that I didn't even realize I was walking until I got halfway across the floor to where the teacher and the girls were standing. Then I got close enough to see that all-alone girl's eyes and she was looking right at me and not even pretending she wasn't. I stopped walking and just stood there looking at her, and I'm not kidding, the lights in the gym brightened up like the sun was shining down from the basketball hoop. And the sunlight sparkled on that girl and made her shine like an angel. Just like in the movies. I always thought they made up that romantic shit but I guess you just think that if you never got struck down by love.

Finally, I noticed that everybody was looking at me, even the teacher, who was this little *gordita* lady with her red hair in a bun and a real tight stretchy black shirt and pants and black high heels with little pink socks just like the ones Letty wears with lace around the tops.

"Welcome to ballroom dance," the lady said. "I'm Mrs. Martinez." She looked down at the clipboard she was holding and then looked at me. "You must be Eduardo Corazon."

"Eddie," I said. I could hardly make myself stop looking at the girl and look at the teacher, who turned out to be

Mexican. From far away, you couldn't tell because of her red hair, but up close you could see that she was born with black hair. But she didn't look like one of those *mexicanas* who change their hair to make themselves look Anglo. She just wanted to look special. I could just see her standing in the back of the Dollar Store, choosing those pink socks and humming a little song and smiling, doing a little cha-cha on the way to the cash register.

At first, Mrs. Martinez made the boys stand in a line across from the girls so she could show us how to make a frame with our arms so we could guide the ladies firmly and smoothly through the box step. She made us dance with her, one at a time, so she could make sure we didn't have noodle arms. Then everybody had to count out loud and do the steps. One and two three. One and two three. The girls all got it right away and so did I. It was real easy, just like doing the *cumbia* in a square, but the other two boys were Anglo and they acted like it was harder than algebra. So Mrs. Martinez called me to the front to demonstrate the steps. I thought she was going to dance with me, but she picked up her clipboard and said, "Now I need a young lady to be your partner." Before Mrs. Martinez could even look at her clipboard, that all-alone girl just walked out and stood in front of me, face to face, so close I could smell her hair which smelled exactly like an angel.

"Why, thank you, Lupe," Mrs. Martinez said, and she smiled like the *viejas* at church when they catch you having

47

lustful thoughts when you're supposed to be listening to the priest. When Mrs. Martinez told Lupe to put her left hand on my right shoulder and told me to put my right hand on Lupe's waist, my inside self started jumping up and down and screaming, "Yes! Yes! Yes!" but outside, I just smiled and stood up as tall as I could to make a good frame for Lupe.

After we did the box step about ten times, Mrs. Martinez clapped her hands and everybody had to find a partner and practice. The girls started giggling again and a couple of them grabbed those Anglo boys real quick while Lupe and I just stood there, holding our frame and our breath, waiting to see if Mrs. Martinez would make us change partners. She didn't make us switch right then, but after we practiced a little bit more, she clapped her hands and said, "Change partners!" and we had to because she was standing right beside us.

Before that class was over, I danced with every single girl. Twenty-three. I touched more girls in that forty-five minutes than I touched in my whole life up until that day. It was one of the best days I ever had, and the best part was that as soon as class was over, Lupe asked me did I know where Mr. McElroy's room was. She just transferred to Bright Horizons, which is why I had never seen her around before. I had been wondering because I would have noticed Lupe even if there had been a million girls at school.

I told Lupe I was going to McElroy's class, so I could walk her over there, and for a minute I even thought about holding out my elbow like when you have to help the *viejas* get down the aisle to their favorite pew. I walked down the hall so proud beside Lupe. She tossed her hair over her shoulder and a little piece touched my cheek and I wished I could put my whole face in her hair and breathe her right inside of me, where I would take care of her forever.

When we got to McElroy's room, he didn't even yell at me for being late because I brought Lupe, but he made me sit in the empty chair in the front row where you have to sit if you get busted for sleeping or passing notes. I didn't even care, because he put Lupe at the desk right behind me. Every couple minutes, I turned just a little bit so McElroy wouldn't notice, until I was sitting sideways and I could see Lupe out of the corner of my eye. And that was the first time I wished English class was longer. I could have sat there forever.

At lunch, I asked Lupe why she was at the alt school because she looked real smart and she didn't dress like a gangbanger or anything, and she said she got kicked out of Rosablanca High because there was this one girl named Cheyenne who kept starting fights with her. I knew exactly which Cheyenne she was talking about. Cheyenne used to be in my class when I was in special ed because she flunked first grade for not being able to read and then the next year she kept banging her head against the wall whenever the teacher asked her to read.

"I don't even know her," Lupe said. "She would just come up and hit me. And she would send her friends over to hit me, too, and then they would tell the teachers that I started it by calling them retards, so nobody believed me. Even when I had witnesses. Finally, I told my father to just pretend he believed them so they would transfer me over here."

I told Lupe that me and my cousins would go and beat those girls down, but she freaked so bad she almost started crying. "No!" she said. "Then they would say I instigated that, too, and I would get in more trouble. I just want to go to school and do my work and graduate so I can go to college." She's going to go to college and be an obstatician so she can help women have babies that don't die from bad nutrition.

I could see why a girl would want to beat Lupe down, especially a big ugly stupid girl. Lupe looks kind of like Salma Hayek and her hair shines even more than Beecher's and she has those perfect round *chichis* that are the exact fit for my hand and a nice fat little butt that looks exactly like an upside-down heart. She looks just as good from the back as she does from the front. Plus, she's probably the smartest girl in class, and maybe even smarter than Harvey Castro.

"Where are you going to college?" Lupe asked me, and I told her I wasn't sure. I didn't tell her I won't even graduate unless I start going to after-school tutoring and even then I'll probably have to go to summer school, too. I told her I was still considering my options and she said, "Good. The more education you have, the more options you have." She sounded just like Beecher, which only proves that Lupe is smart enough to be a teacher even if she's only sixteen. In fact, she's smart enough to figure out how to get out of Bright

Horizons and back to the regular high school if she wanted to, but when I told her that, she said she'd rather stay here where she can work in the computer lab and go as fast as she wants to and just take the final exam after she's done learning something, instead of always having to wait for all the immature obnoxious children who still think school is a big joke.

"You mean like me?" I said and Lupe laughed. "No, not you. You aren't obnoxious. You're just confused. But you're smart."

"How do you know I'm smart?" I said, and Lupe said, "You were smart enough to pick me out of all those girls in ballroom dance class, weren't you?" And she smiled at me because we both know that Lupe is the one who did the picking and I'm the one who got picked.

"Men just think they run things," Lupe told me when we were eating lunch. I was real hungry and for a minute I forgot about making a good impression. I had just shoved half a burrito into my mouth and it was too full of beans and cheese to argue with her.

"Women just let men think they're in charge because it makes you happy," Lupe said. "And you're so cute when you're happy."

Right then, *mi primo* Enrique sneaked up and smacked me on the back which made me spit little bits of cheesy beans all over the cafeteria table. I started coughing and Primo kept pounding me on the back and saying, "You want me to do the Hemlicker on you?"

51

Every time Primo said, "Hemlicker," Lupe said, "It's Heimlich," and Primo said, "Whatever." After the third time, he gave Lupe such a mean look that I pointed to my watch and pointed toward the door so she would just leave and not be late for class. She asked me was I all right and I tried to say, "I'm fine," but that made me cough again.

"See what you did?" Lupe said to Primo. He just balled up his fists and walked away. I didn't try to stop him because he's not even supposed to be on campus on account of he's twenty-five and a bad influence on minors. But sometimes he still comes to check on me and make sure I don't need him to beat somebody up, even though I been telling him for like six years now that I can take care of myself. If he gets caught, he'll probably get arrested on account of having a record, but he's pretty good at not getting caught, plus the principal who kicked him out of school retired and the new principal doesn't know him.

The next time I saw Primo after that, he told me I was whipped and I shouldn't be so nice to Lupe because women don't respect men who are too nice to them. I told him that me and Lupe respect each other and he was just jealous because Lupe was so much smarter than him. He said, "Oh yeah? If she was smart, she would of played you a little bit instead of just jumping into your arms. Besides, if she's so great, she would of already had a boyfriend."

"Haven't you ever heard of love at first sight?" I asked him, and he said, "Haven't you ever heard that guys like the hunt better than the kill? Everybody knows that us guys want what we can't have. If deers just walked up and let people shoot them, nobody would go hunting anymore."

"Yeah, well, I hate hunting," I said. "And I like Lupe and she likes me. And she didn't have a boyfriend because she's serious about school. And besides, she wouldn't pretend not to like somebody that she did like. That would be stupid."

"Whatever," Primo said. "But I still say you're whipped."

I don't think I'm whipped, but even if I am, I don't care because I'm happy. I don't want what I can't have, except if I couldn't have Lupe I would still want her. I wouldn't just forget about her like I forgot about Angela and all those other girls I used to want before I realized it's stupid to want somebody who doesn't want you back. I don't care if all the other guys want what they can't have. I want what I have and I have what I want. I got Lupe.

CHAPTER 8

GIRL + FRIEND

I USUALLY DON'T PAY TOO MUCH ATTENTION TO WHERE WORDS come from because who cares anyway, but today I was thinking that now I know why somebody made up the word *girl-friend*. I only had a couple girlfriends before Lupe. Whenever I had one, she would be my girl but not really my friend. I would like her and want to touch her and think about her before I went to sleep, but if we weren't making out, then I would rather be hanging with Jaime or my cousins, playing ball or shooting pool or just doing nothing. I never wanted to hang out and just do nothing with those girls because it was too boring and they always wanted to have a conversation about something stupid like why didn't I notice their new haircut or what was I thinking.

I liked thinking about those girls more than I liked actually being with them most of the time and back then I couldn't understand why so many guys wanted to get married when their girlfriends weren't even pregnant.

Like my cousins. Most of them are older than me except a couple who are real little like Juanito, and most of the old ones are married, even the real badass ones who were too cool for school. I've been to so many weddings that Mami bought me a special suit to wear. I got more cousins than friends but that's how it is if you're Mexican in New Mexico. You don't need a bunch of friends because if you need something, like your car or your toilet or your roof fixed, you call one of your cousins. Even if they aren't a real cousin but they are married to your brother-in-law's cousin, it still counts. Everybody is somebody's cousin.

As soon as I met Lupe, I started to understand why all my old cousins got married. I used to think it was just so they could have sex all the time, which would be cool, but I never wanted to marry any other girls even though I would have had sex with them if they let me. Lupe won't let me, but I still like to hang around with her because she's like a friend that I want to kiss. Even when we're not kissing or even touching, I still like talking to Lupe because she doesn't ask me what am I thinking, she tells me what she's thinking and then just looks at me. If I say what I'm thinking, she listens, but if I don't say it, she doesn't ask. She just smiles or else just sits real quiet. She's the only person I ever met who can just sit and be quiet and not have to listen to music or watch TV or talk. At first, it made me nervous when she got quiet, but after I got used to it, I started to like it because it calms me down.

Sometimes it feels like Lupe can read my mind. It's probably a lot easier for a girl to read a boy's mind than vice versa because we don't have so many tracks like girls do. We have food and sex and then a couple options, like maybe music or TV or sports or sleeping. A few guys even think about getting an education. But girls have clothes and periods and babies and makeup and does their butt look fat in their new jeans and movies and homework and a hundred other things on their mind all the time. Lupe says she heard some science guy on the radio who said that guys think about sex every ten seconds, which sounds just about right. The guy didn't say how often girls think about sex, but it's probably every ten hours or ten days. Maybe even ten months after they get old and have some babies and a husband and too much work to do.

Primo doesn't get why I like Lupe so much. He says she's too bossy because she's so smart and she isn't afraid of anybody. If you talk some smack to her, she'll smack you back better. But I think the real reason Primo doesn't like Lupe is because she isn't impressed with his Ray-Bans or his flash car or his pockets full of cash. And she says he should have figured out by now that his get-rich-quick plans are never going to work because he always gets busted or else he hooks up with some loser who rips him off or squeals on him to stay out of jail.

The first time Lupe met Primo, I was walking her home from school and he drove up in his new metallic blue Camaro with the chrome spinners and big red flames on the hood. He started flashing his cash, trying to get me to do a little "night project" with him. I told Primo thanks but no thanks. I don't know why he keeps asking me to help him out because I never say yes anymore. He's been asking me for five years and I been saying no all that time, but he keeps asking. He probably thinks he's giving me the opportunity of a lifetime every time, but after I helped him steal this one car, I decided it wasn't worth it. There's no way I'm going to rob a truck full of cell phones or rip off people's car stereos or make fake IDs on the computer. If I was going to take a chance on going to jail, it would have to be for some real smart crime like those guys who steal millions of dollars on the stock market and go to the golf course prison.

Lupe didn't say anything to Primo that first time, but she checked him out real good and after he left, she asked me was he my role model. I said no, he's just my cousin, and she said he looks like a gangster. I told her Primo isn't a gangster because he isn't in a gang, but he is kind of a criminal. She asked me how could somebody be "kind of" a criminal and I explained that he steals car stereos and iPods and stuff like that, but he doesn't sell drugs or mug people. Plus, he mostly steals from rich people who could get new stuff real easy.

Lupe said, "Don't you think rich people feel bad when somebody takes their stuff?" I said, "Yeah, but not as bad as somebody who is poor and can't go get some new stuff." Lupe said stealing is stealing, period, and you can't be "kind of" a criminal, just like you can't be "kind of" pregnant. Either you are or you aren't. I didn't say anything after that because it's real hard to win any argument with a smart girl whose father is a lawyer and I knew I wasn't going to win that one.

Lupe says Primo is unethical and lazy because he steals instead of getting some kind of legal job. If anybody else insulted my family like that, I wouldn't like them, but Lupe doesn't say that stuff to make Primo look bad or to make me not like him. She just has real high ethics. I told her she's only half right because maybe Primo doesn't have such good ethics but he isn't lazy. He works real hard at being a criminal. Lupe said if he worked half as hard at a job as he did at being slick and ripping people off, he'd probably make a lot more money and he wouldn't have to worry about going to prison if he gets caught.

Primo can't work at a regular job where he has a boss who can yell at him and he can't punch the guy. He always gets fired after one or two days. It must run in the family or something because Papi has a hard time working at a job where somebody tells him what to do and what to wear and when to eat lunch and he better watch his mouth or else. If he didn't have Mami and us kids to take care of, he would probably be in jail for fighting or else working out on some ranch as a cowboy who doesn't have to pretend to respect dumb people just to get a paycheck. And I'm the same way, which is why I have so many problems in school. If they would just let you read the books and take the tests, I probably would have graduated by now or at least I would like school. But they can't just let you learn. They have to make up all those stupid rules, like you can't wear your baseball cap sideways and you can't listen to your music on a headset even if you have good grades and you aren't bothering anybody, and you can't walk around with your shoes untied or your pants sagging which isn't hurting anybody unless you fall down and then it's your own fault so you can't sue them anyways.

Lupe loves school. She doesn't care how many rules they make up. She just goes around thinking about her plan of being a doctor. And she doesn't care if she's popular, either. She's the only girl I ever met who didn't care if the other girls liked her or if they said bad things about her. She only cares if they hit her because then she gets suspended and that interferes with her academic plan of getting a perfect GPA so she can go to whatever college she picks instead of whatever college picks her.

I remember this one day we were coming out of the gym after ballroom dance class and a couple guys looked at Lupe too long and then one of them said something about dancing. I couldn't hear exactly what he said, but I got his message. I was thinking I should go smack that guy, but Lupe read my mind and said don't waste your time because who cares about those people and they probably can't dance, anyway, so they're just jealous.

I told Lupe I don't care if other kids don't like me but if some guy disrespects me, I have to hit him if I want to maintain my reputation. She said, "Why?" and I said, "Because," but I didn't have anything to go with it. When you say "Because" and you don't add anything, you sound like a little kid, but Lupe didn't laugh at me. She just said, "I don't worry about what people think unless they are my friends and I respect them."

I wished I could be like her because I don't really respect too many people except Jaime and Henry Dominguez and a couple old people and some of my cousins. If I didn't have to worry about what everybody else thinks, it would make life a lot easier. I told Lupe maybe I would try having her attitude and see how it worked, but even if I said I didn't care what people think about me, I would probably still care. It's one thing to say something and another thing to do it.

"High school is an artificial social construct," Lupe told me. "You only get to choose your friends from among the people your own age who live within a certain geographic area. Maybe there isn't anybody in that group who can appreciate you. Except me, of course." She stood on her tiptoes and kissed me on the nose, which I liked, but I still looked around to make sure nobody else saw.

"After we get out of school, we can choose our friends from all the people in the world," Lupe said. "We might meet somebody from Egypt or Japan or Santa Fe who is eighty-five or eight, but we won't care where they live or how old they are or how they dress. We'll just care about who they are. We can be friends with people who are interesting and who think we're interesting."

That's why Lupe is my girl and my friend and my girl-friend. Not just because she's smart and beautiful and interesting, but she thinks I'm interesting, too. Not because of what I do or what I have, but just because of who I am.

CHAPTER 9

MARGARITAS EN MÉXICO

WHEN *MI PRIMO* ENRIQUE FIRST TRIED TO GET ME TO DITCH school and go to Mexico with him, I said no because I been doing pretty good on turning over my new leaf. I figured he was just going there to drink margaritas and visit this girl he knows there named Adelberta who dances in a nightclub which is good because she probably looks a lot better in the dark, but he said he was going to the dentist to get his new tooth. He opened his mouth and pulled his lip down so I could see this one broken tooth. He said he broke it eating some peanuts. I didn't remind him that he already told me this guy broke it with a beer bottle after Primo sold him some broken speakers for his car stereo. I just told Primo I didn't like Juárez and he didn't need me to help him get a tooth glued on.

"Yes, I do," Primo said. "What if they give me a shot and knock me out and steal my wallet and my truck? And then they might sell me as a sex slave because I'm so *guapo*. You know you can't trust those *méxicanos*, muchacho." He tipped his head down and grinned at me over the top of his sunglasses. I told him have a nice time and let me know when he got back.

"Come on, Preem," he said. "I'm serious. I could get sick from the anesthetic. You don't want me to die in a car crash, do you? Then you'd have to put a big white cross and a bunch of plastic flowers beside the road and you'd have to go visit me all the time and it's a long drive, especially with gas prices these days. Plus, I'm talking Palomas, not Juárez."

I started to say no again, but he said, "Hey, I'm family. You can't let me down."

I knew if I got caught and told Papi I did it for family, he would still be mad, but he probably wouldn't even ground me. And Lupe was on a field trip to visit New Mexico State to see if she wanted to go to college there in case she didn't get accepted at some place good, so she wouldn't find out and get mad as long as I didn't tell Jaime who would tell Lena who can't keep her mouth shut.

"If I go, I don't want to visit any hookers," I told Primo, "just go to the dentist and come right back."

"I keep telling you Berta isn't a hooker," he said. "She's an exotic dancer. There's a big difference, which you would know if you knew anything about women. If they give it away, they aren't *putas*. They're just friendly, like me. I never charge women. I could probably make a lot of money if I did, though."

He grinned at me again, so I said, "Are you high? Because if you are, I'm not riding with you." I was standing on the curb, a couple blocks from school. Primo was sitting in his old truck with the engine idling. He sat up straight and stopped smiling.

"Yo, bro, I'm straight as an arrow. But you can drive if it makes you feel better." He got out of his truck and walked around and moved me away from the passenger door. He got inside, put on his seat belt and looked at me real serious until I got behind the wheel.

We just cranked up the speakers and didn't talk too much until we got to Cruces. We stopped to get some gas and a couple bottles of iced tea which I thought Primo would add something to, but he didn't. He just climbed back into the passenger seat and waited until we were on I-10 and then he said, "I never thanked you for not ratting me out that day."

He didn't have to tell me which day. We both knew.

I didn't say anything. I didn't say I was too scared to tell anybody. I was too scared to do anything. I didn't eat or talk for a couple days. I even got a fever. Mami took me to the doctor and he said I probably had laryngitis or something. He said sometimes kids yell so much when they're playing outside that they lose their voice. Nothing to worry about, he said. After a couple days, I could eat a little bit, but I had nightmares every night for a whole year. I tried to erase that day from my brain and I never said anything about it to anybody, including Primo. He never said anything about it, either. Not for eight years up till now. I thought Primo must have forgot about it, even though I didn't, but it isn't the kind of thing you could forget, especially if you were the one who pulled the trigger.

Primo stared out his window at the Black Range Mountains, which look green and blue in the daylight. "You know why I never told you why I shot that guy?" He waited a minute, but I didn't answer him. I didn't even shake my head. I just sat there wishing I wasn't in the truck with him. I was wishing that I was in school listening to McElroy talk about Shakespeare or something, which would have surprised McElroy even more than it surprised me.

"You were too little, that's why. I didn't want you to know the bad things that some people will do. I'm still not going to tell you because maybe you'll never find out which would be good. But you remember that girl who got pregnant and told everybody it was my baby but I said it wasn't?"

"Yeah." I did remember that girl. An Anglo girl named Debbie with long blond hair and skinny legs. She was a senior and Primo was only a sophomore. She stayed in school until she got so fat that they made her quit because they thought other kids would want to have babies if they hung around with her which is so stupid. Maybe girls think it's cool to look at a fat pregnant belly, but guys don't. If they put a pregnant girl in every class, I bet a lot of guys would start using condoms.

"It was my baby," Primo said. "The prettiest little girl you ever saw. But I was too young to be a dad. I was a *pendejo*, I admit that. But she was the one who seduced me." He stopped talking for a second and looked out the window some more. "When she found a new boyfriend, I thought, Good, now I'm off the hook. No child support, no hassles from her. But that guy was *puro diablo*. He . . ."

He took off his sunglasses and rubbed his eyes and put the glasses back on.

"I'm not going to tell you what he did to that little girl, but I promise if somebody did that to your kid, you'd shoot them. Anybody would." He punched the dashboard and then rubbed his knuckles.

"How come you think the cops never came looking for me?" He looked at me hard.

"I don't know."

"Because they knew what he did, except nobody couldn't prove it," Primo said. "Even the cops don't care if you kill some guy like him. That's the kind of *basura* you don't need the cops or the courts to decide anything about. Everybody knows the right thing to do. So I did it."

I got a sick feeling when he said that because I remembered sitting in that car, smoking that cigarette, and then shitting my pants after Primo pulled the trigger. I picked up my iced tea and chugged the rest of the bottle.

"Hey." Primo waited until I looked over at him and then he said, "I'm sorry you saw that. I'm sorry I didn't wait. But everybody told me that guy was headed for the border and when I saw him I knew it was my only chance. I had to do it. You understand that?"

"Yeah," I said. "I probably would of killed him, too, if it was me."

"I didn't kill him. Just blew his face off. When they took him to the emergency room, he thought he was dying, so he started confessing about everything he ever did. He didn't wait until there was a priest. He confessed to whoever would listen . . . doctors, nurses, cops. After they fixed his face, they threw his ass in jail and locked him up."

"For good?"

"Who knows," Primo said. "He told everybody his friends on the outside would kill me, but nobody did. Somebody probably killed him in jail by now. Maybe not. Maybe someday I'll walk out of some building and take a bullet in the back. Or I'll drive past the wrong corner and find a drive-by waiting for me."

He reached over and punched me on the arm. Not too hard. And he kept his hand there for a little while.

"You never know if today is your last day," he said. "That's why I say enjoy yourself. The sun is shining, the margaritas are icy, and the women are hot."

I drank a margarita that day, and Primo drank three, and then we went to the dentist and got his tooth glued back on. The dentist smelled his breath and laughed and said Primo didn't need any anesthetic.

On the way to the dentist, we saw this Indian-looking

lady with two little kids, and they were all dressed like those old-time posters of the *Indios* with long black braids and a white blouse with ruffles and a real puffy skirt with red and blue and yellow parts. The lady was real short, not even five feet tall, and she didn't look at us, just opened the door of this big pink store where you can buy lunch and margaritas and all kinds of tourist junk. She held the door open and stood there and didn't look up and didn't hold out her hand or ask for money or anything. And her two little girls just stood there, too, looking at the ground. They looked exactly like the woman except smaller, like those dolls that Letty has where you open the big doll and there's another one inside just like it and you open that one and there's a littler one.

Those little girls looked so tired and old and sad and I thought they were probably hungry, so I started to hand the lady a five-dollar bill, but Primo grabbed my arm and stopped me. He reached into the front pocket of his jeans and pulled out a couple of quarters and tossed them to her. When we got inside, he said, "Didn't you see those guys?"

I said, "What guys?" and he said, "Those guys hanging out across the street."

I looked back out through the door and saw a bunch of guys with dusty jeans and boots and old crooked cowboy hats smoking cigarettes or drinking Tecates, leaning against the building or squatting by the curb, but nobody talking. They looked the same as guys everywhere who don't have jobs or wives or girlfriends who make them come home and mow the lawn or fix the windows.

"If you give that *pobrecita* money, they'll take it from her," Primo said. He walked through the store past a bunch of silver jewelry and paper flowers and giant pots into another room, where the restaurant was. When the lady at the counter asked him did we need menus, he said, "Nachos y margaritas, por favor."

When the waitress brought our bill, I asked her for some quarters. As soon as she walked away, Primo asked me did I need quarters to buy a condom in the bathroom in case we got lucky on the way out of town.

"Ha-ha," I said. I knew he knew what I wanted the quarters for.

"You got any ones?" Primo asked me. I nodded and he flipped his wallet shut and shoved it into his front pocket, where he keeps it because he wears his jeans real tight and he says if somebody can get their hand into his front pocket without him knowing, that will be the day somebody loses their *cojones*. "Give me the bills."

I handed him eight singles and he handed one back to me and told me to stick it in my front pocket. Then he took the rest and folded them into squares and put them into the palm of his hand and curled his fingers around them. "Can you see them?"

"No," I said.

"Okay, here's what you do. You look in that little basket of bracelets that lady has sitting on the sidewalk. You look through them all real careful, checking out the colors and how big they are. And you mix them up real good, and while you're mixing, you put those bills into the bottom of that basket. Then you pick out two or three bracelets and you stand up and pull that dollar out of your pocket and give it to her. Those guys will see the dollar and they'll probably leave her alone because it's not that much money. But if she's smart, she'll move on down the street with her basket and stick the rest of that money someplace secret."

"Why can't we give her a couple fives instead of all those ones?" I said.

"Hello." Primo knocked me on the head like a door. "She has to spend the money, right? If she goes into a store and buys something with a five-dollar bill, then whoever is watching will see she has money. They'll follow her and take whatever she has left. If she just has ones, she can spend them one at a time and hide the rest."

I asked Primo did he figure out that plan from his own experience or did somebody teach him and he said, "What do you think, muchacho?"

CHAPTER 10

LUPE FULL OF GRACE

I CAN'T BELIEVE IT. I ACTUALLY WROTE SOME POEMS. BEECHER tried to get me to write some last year after she caught me reading this one library book that had a bunch of poems by Gary Soto, but I wouldn't do it just like I wouldn't sign up for ballroom dance back then. But last week when Lupe said she thought poets were deep, I decided I better give it a try—especially since T.J. Ritchie wrote a poem that Mr. McElroy typed up and sent to a magazine because he said it was so good. I can't have T.J. going around looking deeper than me, especially in front of Lupe.

When I told Lupe I was thinking about writing a poem, she clapped her hands and kissed me on the mouth, right in the hallway. Then I had to do it, except I couldn't think of a subject. So I looked it up in our literature book where there's a chapter on poetry. In the writing assignment part it said anything could inspire a poem, it doesn't have to be nature or love or death or big important things. You can just look around at the world and paint word pictures of what you see, like a red wheelbarrow. So I looked around McElroy's room at the punks and stoners and assorted losers, and the bulletin boards and all the lame posters that are supposed to inspire you because they have a picture of an airplane crashing through a bunch of clouds and a quotation underneath the airplane that is supposed to make you want to be a successful person instead of a high school dropout. Then I wrote two poems, just like that. Here they are:

ALTERNATIVE EDUCATION

I read a quotation that said
"When the student is ready, the teacher appears"
and I was thinking sometimes
I need to learn something
except I'm not really ready
but the teacher appears anyway
so I ditch that class
and go smoke behind the gym.
Most of the teachers don't care if I'm gone
but one teacher will follow me out to the gym
and she won't bust me for smoking
or tell me how cigarettes can kill me.

Instead, she'll watch me smoke a little while.
Then she'll hand me a flute and say
"Why don't you play me a song?"

Okay. That was number one. I still haven't decided whether I like it or not because it has such a weird ending. But I didn't even make up that ending. It just came out of my pencil.

Number two I wrote because of this one girl with purple and green hair on one side of her head and no hair on the other side because she shaved it all off. She has about ten earrings in her ears and a little bone in her eyebrow and a diamond in her nose and something stuck in her tongue. She wears real short T-shirts so you can see the rings in her navel and she has weird bumps on her chest so she must have some in her nipples, too. When Letty got her ears pierced, she went around smiling all the time, checking herself out in the mirror and admiring her earrings. But that pierced girl never smiles. She's the saddest person I ever saw, but she doesn't go around crying or anything. Mostly she swears at everybody. I don't have a good title for her poem, so right now I'm just calling it "Pierce Everything."

PIERCE EVERYTHING

Punk up your hair or shave your head
Pierce your eyebrows and your nipples and
    your lips and your soul

So the hate and the hurt can ooze out of you
through a million tiny holes

I got some tears in my eyes after I wrote that one, but lucky for me nobody saw because the bell rang for lunch while I was writing and everybody except Lupe ran out of the room, including McElroy who always goes jogging during lunch in some baggy brown shorts. Lupe stayed at her desk, but she wasn't looking at me. She was copying down the assignment from the whiteboard and she had her head bent down close to her notebook. It almost looked like she was praying and her hair fell down and hid her face like a shiny black satin curtain. And Lupe became my next poem.

LUPE FULL OF GRACE

I wish I could be Lupe's rosary
so she could hold me in her hands
and tangle me up in her fingers
and press me to her lips
and pray me into being a good man
one bead at a time

After I wrote that, I felt like I had turned into a poem myself. I felt as light as a piece of paper, like I could float right up to the ceiling. I copied that poem over real neat and tore the page out of my notebook and folded it over and over, like the little kids do, until it was a tiny little square. I wrote Lupe's initials on it and put it in my pocket and carried it around with me until after school when I pretended to tickle Lupe and I stuck it inside her bra and held her hands so she couldn't get it out. When I finally let go, she hit me in the head with her purse and called me a *pachuco*, but I didn't even care. I just smiled, thinking of my poem sitting so close to Lupe's heart.

CHAPTER 11

SECRET READERS

AFTER LUPE READ MY POEM, SHE CRIED. THEN SHE TOLD ME I should be a writer because if you can write something that makes people cry then you have the gift. I told Lupe maybe I had a little tiny gift. Maybe only she would cry from reading my poems and not other people, so she said, "Let's show them to Mr. McElroy and see what he thinks," and I said, "Not."

"You shouldn't be afraid," Lupe said. "He's not a very good teacher, but he's a nice man. And he wouldn't laugh at you, if that's what you're thinking."

"I'm not afraid he would laugh at me," I said, except that is exactly what I was thinking. "I just don't want to show them to nobody but you."

We were sitting on the bench outside the main office

eating lunch, where most kids don't like to hang out because it's too close to the principal. There are other places where it would be more private but I don't trust myself to be in private places with Lupe at school. When we're in the same class, sometimes I have to get myself kicked out because sometimes I can't sit down when Lupe's in the same room with me—if you know what I mean. I have to get out of the room just so I can breathe.

"Your poem is better than T.J. Ritchie's poem that got sent to the magazine," Lupe said. "He showed it to me. Yours is way better."

I didn't like T.J. showing his poem to my girlfriend, but at least she liked mine better than his. Unless she was just trying to give me self-esteem which she thinks is so important if you want to succeed in life. Beecher was always talking about self-esteem, too, and how you can program your brain to succeed because your brain doesn't know when you're lying. Like if you keep telling yourself, "I am an intelligent, successful person," your brain will believe you even though your brain is sitting right there where it could see that you're a stupid loser if it took a good look.

I believed Lupe liked my poem better, though, because she never lies to me even though *mi primo* Enrique says you can never trust a woman. Plus, I read T.J.'s poem and it wasn't that good even though it was better than some of the poems in our literature book.

Everybody acted all surprised when they found out T.J.

wrote a real poem because T.J. makes a big deal out of not living up to his potential and being disruptive and antisocial. But he's a secret reader, just like me, except he's even more secret than I am. If somebody asks me do I like to read, I say, "Yeah," and then I give them a look that tells them they better not ask me what I like to read because this ain't Oprah's book club. But T.J. pretends he doesn't even know how to read. If a teacher tries to make him read out loud in class, T.J. will either read like he's in kindergarten, pushing his big dirty finger across the page and reading one word at a time or else he'll say, "Reading sucks," and he'll say *suck* real dirty so it sounds like the other *uck* word, so the teacher will send him to the office for using inappropriate language.

T.J. reads real books when nobody is looking, though. I caught him myself. Once, I saw him reading a book behind the bleachers when we were both cutting first-period math. When I walked past, T.J. dropped the book on the ground and put his foot on it like he didn't know it was there and he asked me did I have a cigarette. I said sorry, I just smoked my last one, even though I don't smoke because I'm not stupid enough to think lung cancer is cool just because they put a camel or a cowboy on the commercial. Right then, one of the security guards slammed open the gym door and then let it slam shut real loud to let us know that if we didn't get back to class we'd get busted. So T.J. left that book laying right in the dirt. I got a bathroom pass the next period and took a little detour behind the bleachers on my way and that book was still there. It wasn't porn or a comic book, like I expected. It was a real book—*The Curious Incident of the Dog in the Night-Time*. I read the first page or two just to see what kind of a book would have a title like that and it turned out to be about this kid who everybody thought was stupid, except he was really smart in some ways. Like he couldn't have a conversation with anybody but he could multiply real big numbers in his head like that guy in *Rain Man*. He reminded me of a lot of the kids in special ed who aren't as stupid as the teachers think they are.

The next thing I knew I read the whole book, so I must of sat out there for a couple of hours. I got detention for cutting but I didn't care because I wanted some quiet time to think about that book. I had never read anything like it before. That weekend, I went to the bookstore and asked the lady did she have any more books by the guy who wrote that one. She said no but she asked me if I wanted to try another book with an unusual title and she gave me *The Lone Ranger and Tonto Fistfight in Heaven* by the same Indian guy who wrote the story that Beecher read us. After I read those two books, I realized there are two kinds of books in the world— the boring kind they make you read in school and the interesting kind that they won't let you read in school because then they would have to talk about real stuff like sex and divorce and is there a God and if there isn't then what happens when you die, and how come the history books have so many lies in them. They make us read the boring books so the teachers just have to talk about safe stuff like amoebas and tsetse flies and the hypotenuse of a triangle and all those things which nobody cares about in real life.

The warning bell rang to let everybody know it was time to stop eating lunch and enjoying themselves and get back to earning an education, so Lupe gathered up all her stuff and shoved it in her backpack. I was so busy watching her move because she is so graceful, like a flamenco dancer with hands that can become a flying dove or a flower opening up its petals, so I didn't realize Lupe also put my notebook with the poems into her backpack until she said, "I have your poems and I'm going to show them to Mr. McElroy unless you get down on your knees and beg me to give them back to you."

I would do anything for Lupe. I would kill for her. But there is no way I get on my knees for anything—except to ask Lupe to marry me, which I'm going to do someday but not until I have a good job so I can take care of her. I told Lupe go ahead because I didn't care if she showed my poems to McElroy but don't tell him I wrote them. I don't want him reading them out loud in front of everybody and saying I wrote them because I have a reputation to maintain. Lupe laughed and gave me back my notebook.

"I wasn't really going to show them to anybody," she said. "They're too personal. I just wanted to see how brave you really are." She squeezed my bicep and pretended to be surprised at how buff I am in spite of being so skinny. "Ooh. He's smart and sensitive and strong *and* fearless," she said. She ran her fingers up my arm and touched my lips with her finger. Then she put the finger on her own lips and kissed it which made me dizzy. And the next thing I knew, I was sitting in McElroy's class where we had to write a five-paragraph essay.

"Tell me what you're going to tell me," he said. "Then, tell me. Then tell me what you told me. It's simple."

It's simple, all right. And boring. And stupid. And pointless. But you have to write the essay to pass the exam so you can graduate and the teacher won't get fired. I was going to write about music and how it can make you smart, which is something that Beecher taught us. She said if you listen to certain music, you get smarter. And some music makes plants grow better. I looked it up on the Internet to see if she was just playing us, but she was telling the truth. There was all kinds of articles and scientific reports about how classical music makes you smart but heavy metal and rap can screw up your head. I stopped listening to rap after that. I never liked it much anyway, but I liked driving around with my homies with the windows down, playing rap music loud enough to break your head, wearing shades, and staring down all the old people who would roll up their car windows real fast like they were scared we were going to carjack them right in front of TacoTime. I believe those articles because if you listen to metal or rap really loud, like in a car that has sixteen batteries in the trunk to juice the speakers, after a while you get a feeling like you just won a fight or kissed a girl or something, except you didn't do anything. You get this rush, like chemicals in your blood, and you feel like you had some real feelings except you didn't have to feel them.

That's what I was going to write about but McElroy said we had to write about his topic, which was politics. I used to didn't care about politics because it doesn't make any difference to me if the president wears a red necktie or a blue one. Then I heard the president giving a speech on television and he said he doesn't listen to his father because his father doesn't tell him what to do. So I figured he might be all right because I don't listen to Papi, neither. But then the president said he talks to God and God tells him what to do. I kept expecting somebody to jump up and scream, "It's *Saturday Night Live!*" but it was for real. So I wondered how come they don't make him stop being president. Because if the president of some other country went on TV and said he gets messages from Allah or some kind of foreign god who doesn't speak English, Americans would freak out and think he was a lunatic and assassinate him or put economic sanctions on him. So, I looked the president up on the Internet and that's when I found this Web site called Common Dreams, and that's where I read that one of the new political plans is to get rid of all the Mexicans.

Everybody knows the Anglos are nervous about Mexicans having so many kids and taking over the country. But they didn't really think it could happen until one day they counted up the people and California was half Hispanic. New Mexico is probably more than half Hispanic, too, but New Mexicans aren't stupid enough to stand still and let people count us. And we know how to get along in New Mexico. If you want to rub elbows with mostly Anglos and speak English, move down to Cruces. If you want to speak Spanish, move over to Deming or up to Española. If you like to mix it up a little, then you got a bunch of little towns in the middle to pick from, like Tularosa, Socorro, and Truth or Consequences.

I don't blame the Anglos for being worried about so many Mexicans because they know payback is a bitch and we got a lot of payback coming. And if us Mexicans ever joined up with our Indian and black brothers, the Anglos would have to circle those wagon trains for real. But we wouldn't kill the Anglos which is what they think. We wouldn't torture them, neither, or make them slaves or make them speak a different language because we know how much that kind of stuff sucks. We wouldn't rape all the white women, either. We wouldn't have to. A lot of white women like dark men. They know we like sports, just like the *güeros*, but the brown brothers won't pass up a hot woman to watch a game on TV. We know how to hit the RECORD button and watch the game later.

So, we won't kill the *güeros*. We'll just put them to work. We'll make them be the cooks and the janitors and the car washers and the lawn mowers and the sewer diggers. We'll pay them two dollars an hour and fire them if they take a day off to take their kid to the hospital. We'll talk to them in Spanish and if they don't understand us, we'll say it louder and slower, and shake our heads because how stupid can you be not to be able to speak such a simple language. In Spanish, you say the letters in all the words just like they look. *A* is always *ah*, and *E* is always *ay*, and *I* is always *eee*. We don't have six different ways to say the same letters, like *dough* and *thought* and *through* and *tough* which all have *o-u* but different pronunciations, so that when you're trying to learn English you sound stupid no matter how smart you are.

We'll make the Anglos live in falling-down trailers and work in the fields picking chiles fourteen hours a day even when it's a hundred and ten degrees. We'll feel real sorry for them and maybe even appreciate them. We'll say, "I don't know how you can stand the heat. You people are so strong," and we'll pretend we believe they have a choice. We'll pretend we like them, too. We'll make statues of cute little round, fat Anglos and put them on our front doorsteps for decorations.

But we won't let the Anglos take care of our kids. We don't need day care and nannies because Mexicans haven't forgotten their families like Anglos have. We take care of each other's kids and we take care of each other. *Como mi primo* Enrique always says, "In Mexico, family is still family. If one person has a job, everybody eats. And everybody takes care of the little ones—*tías y tíos, primas y primos, abuelas y abuelos. Todos aman a los niños.*"

I wrote all that in my essay so I might get an F. It depends on whether McElroy grades it on how well I wrote it, like capital letters and punctuation and good spelling and grammar, or if he grades it on whether he doesn't like my opinion. You never know about teachers. Sometimes they fool you. Like Beecher. She fooled me a lot until I finally figured out that she was smart on a higher level than most people.

I don't care if McElroy gives me a bad grade on my essay. I have to go to summer school anyway because I cut too much before I met Lupe and turned over my new leaf. Even if Mc-Elroy flunks my essay, it doesn't matter because I know it's a good essay and I'm glad I wrote it.

CHAPTER 12

GARRULOUS GABE AND SILENT SLIM

MCELROY MUST HAVE EITHER GOT A GIRLFRIEND, OR MAYBE A boyfriend, I'm not sure which. But somebody must have got ahold of him because a couple weeks ago he showed up at school looking like one of those loser straight guys from that show where the gay guys teach the loser guy how to dress cool and act right and fix up his house so a girl would want to spend more than two minutes visiting him. McElroy had a buzz cut and an earring and he must have got contacts, too, because the pink glasses were gone. Instead of khaki pants and a polo shirt, he had on a black shirt and some Wranglers and a pair of black snakeskin Tony Lamas, which aren't cheap.

McElroy must have been reading some of the same books

that Beecher read, too, because he didn't teach his normal way where everybody took a nap while he talked and then we did some stupid pointless assignment. He handed out some blank contracts and told us we had to fill them out. There was a space to put your name and the date and then spaces to describe your project and list the names of your partners, if you didn't want to work by yourself. And at the bottom it said that you had to sign the contract to show that you knew when the assignment was due because if you didn't do it, you would flunk English for the semester.

"This is your opportunity to demonstrate your intelligence," McElroy said. "You are going to design a project to demonstrate the skills that are not normally appreciated in school. There are many forms of intelligence that enable you to be successful in your professional and personal lives, but they cannot be taught or evaluated in a school setting."

Everybody was looking at McElroy for a change, partly because he looked so different and partly because nobody knew what he was talking about.

"There is emotional intelligence, spatial intelligence, physical intelligence," McElroy said. "For example, you may be very good at negotiating deals, writing songs, creating complex recipes, or singing or dancing. This project will allow you to earn credit for your unique set of skills."

Teeny White raised her hand. "Can we write a book report?"

McElroy nodded. "That's an option. But I would prefer

that you create a project that transcends the traditional research-and-regurgitate method."

"Hey, that means puke," Henry Dominguez said. He grabbed his stomach and pretended to chuck.

"You know what I mean," McElroy said. "I don't want you to tell me what somebody else thinks. I want you to tell me what you think. The only restrictions are that you cannot present something that is hate-based, pornographic, or violent. And all projects have to be presented to the class."

"You mean we have to give a speech?" Curtis Coleman practically hollered because he stutters whenever he has to give a speech in front of the class.

"No, you don't have to give a speech," McElroy said. He sat down on the top of his desk and looked around at us. "I can't believe you aren't excited about this project. This is a chance for you to be creative, show your stuff, get out of the old boring schoolwork rut."

Teeny White said if you have to present to the class then it's a speech, isn't it, and McElroy said not a *speech* speech, like reading off a paper or memorizing something. But you could show how to build a model airplane, or how to cut somebody's hair, or take care of fish in an aquarium, or you could write a poem and say it to the class, or make your own television commercial, or you could sing a song or play a trumpet or draw a picture or give a dance demonstration.

"Can I do a rap song?" Phillip Finley asked, and everybody laughed because he's so white he glows in the dark and he's not Eminem.

McElroy held up his hands to tell us to shut up which we wouldn't have done before he had that haircut, but this time it worked. "No laughing at other people. That's an unbreakable rule. You are going to get a grade on your presentation, and you're going to grade each other's projects, but you're also going to get a grade as an audience member. I expect you to show some respect for each other." He clapped his hands real loud like that would motivate us. "Now, let's start brainstorming your projects. You have to hand in that contract to get out the door when the bell rings."

I knew Lupe was going to want to do a dance demonstration because the second McElroy mentioned dancing, she looked over at me real quick. I shook my head but Lupe doesn't give up that easy. As soon as McElroy said to start planning, she came over to my desk and said, "Come on, Eddie, let's dance," and I said, "Come on, Lupe, let's not." She said, "Yeah, it'll be fun," and I said, "No way," and she said, "Way," and then I said, "If you really liked me, you wouldn't pressure me to do something I don't want to do."

Lupe flopped down in the chair next to mine and punched me on the arm. "That's not fair."

"Then how come it's fair for you to say that when I want us to get naked?" I asked her.

"Shh!" Lupe said and looked around to make sure nobody was listening which they weren't because everybody except the kiss-asses were all busy trying to think of some way to do a presentation where they didn't have to talk in front of the class too much. "That's different and you know it."

"No, it isn't," I said. I had been kind of pissed when Lupe said the girls' gym teacher told them to say, "If you loved me, you wouldn't ask me to do things I don't want to do," because you can't talk a girl into doing stuff if somebody puts ideas like that into her head. But it turned out to be a pretty good idea for me, too.

"There's no way I'm going to dance in front of the class, so don't ask me anymore," I said, and Lupe said, "Fine," and I said, "Fine," and she huffed off to find Lena who is a reasonable person who isn't afraid of a little peer pressure. That got Jaime off the hook, so he came over and we tried to figure out what kind of intelligence we have that we could show to other people without looking too stupid.

Jaime isn't shy because he's an altar boy and he has to sing in front of all the people in church every week. He said we should make a television show and I said how can you make a show with only two people and besides, I didn't want to talk in front of everybody. He said we could be those movie review guys who talk about thumbs-up or thumbs-down.

"We can show some parts of the movies which will take up most of our time," Jaime said, "and then we can just say a little bit about the movies. And if we show something sexy, all the guys will give us a good grade and some of the girls will, too."

We picked the scene in *Blue in the Face* where the sexy girlfriend takes off her dress while she's singing in front of the mirror and pretending to be a tiger for the boys, and the beginning of *Finding Nemo*, Jaime's all-time favorite movie. We named ourselves Garrulous Gabe and Silent Slim. *Garrulous* was one of our vocabulary words, so we knew McElroy would be impressed. And we figured he'd be even more impressed because we used irony in the names. We wrote a script and I played Garrulous Gabe except I hardly talked and Jaime played Silent Slim, who talked and talked and talked.

We acted like we were all cool and not nervous, but when project day came up, me and Jaime were next to last and we were hoping we would run out of time before it was our turn, but McElroy dinged a bell and made people shut up if they were taking too long, so everybody stayed right on schedule.

At first, I got pretty nervous when McElroy announced us, but Jaime just got up and shoved two desks together to make a big desk like on television. Then we put on neckties over our T-shirts and everybody laughed which made me feel better. If you start out with a joke and nobody laughs, then everything goes downhill after that.

We showed the scene from *Finding Nemo* first and Jaime gave it two thumbs up and made up a whole bunch of real convincing stuff about how it was a heartwarming movie that the whole family could enjoy together. I gave it a thumbs-down and just said, "Boring." Then we showed the *Blue in the Face* scene and Jaime gave it one thumbs-up and one thumbs-down because there was too much talking and too much sex for kids to watch it. I gave it two thumbs up and said, "Check it out."

We got half a standing ovation from the kids and Mc-Elroy gave us an A which was pretty good since I only had to say four words in front of the class.

The last project was Lalo Peña. When McElroy said push all the desks back against the wall because Lalo was going to give us a kung fu demonstration, everybody started laughing because Lalo's so short and round and wears glasses. Just like Harvey Castro. We all thought it was a big joke that Lalo and Harvey were taking kung fu classes. Harvey's mother used to ask my mother did I want to sign up for kung fu with Harvey because it might help me get some discipline, but I always said, "No thanks."

Everybody stopped laughing when Lalo walked into the room in that white uniform with bare feet because he was wearing a black belt and no glasses and his face looked real different. The black belt turned out to be a real black belt. He didn't say anything, just put his hands together in front of his chest and closed his eyes and breathed real deep and then bowed and said something that sounded like Chinese. Then, boom, he opened his eyes and started punching and kicking all over the place. He could kick higher than his head and when he slapped his hand against his arm it sounded loud enough to make you jump a little bit. We all moved back against the wall so he wouldn't accidentally kill us.

After a couple minutes, Lalo stopped punching and kicking and bowed again. He kneeled down and put his forehead on the floor and then he sat back and told us about how kung fu is not about fighting and hitting other people, it's about not fighting or hitting other people. He said it's about putting all your power into your brain so you could control your body and your energy and deflect bad energy from coming at you. Then he stood up and did some more punching and kicking and nobody said one word and when he finished, everybody clapped so loud. We would have gave him a giant standing ovation even if we weren't already standing up.

After that, nobody messed with Lalo anymore, even the kids from other classes who didn't see his demonstration because when you can do the kind of stuff that Lalo did in front of our class everybody hears about it. And all us guys realized Lalo or Harvey could have kicked our asses so fast if they wanted to which was why they never fight. They don't have to fight. Like if you're really really smart, you don't have to go around showing people how smart you are. Like Beecher. You just know it in your heart and it makes you too strong to care about what other people think.

CHAPTER 13

GOOGLING GOD

TODAY MCELROY GOT IN BIG TROUBLE FOR LETTING US TALK about God and homosexuals in class except he didn't let us. He just couldn't stop us. I didn't do any talking. But just listening was enough to give me a headache from trying to figure out who was right and who was wrong. We were supposed to be learning how to do analogies but as soon as McElroy said who wants to try number one, T.J. Ritchie said something stupid just to be funny and this kid beside him who is almost as big as T.J. said, "Shut up, you fag," and Curtis Coleman hollered, "Don't be so homophobic!" McElroy tapped his ruler on his desk and said, "That's enough," but T.J. jumped up and said, "Who you calling homophobic?" and Curtis said, "Just about everybody in this pathetic excuse for a town." Curtis is a intellectual who moved here from

California last year and he's always talking about how much better it is in California. Usually we don't argue with him because we know he's probably right, except sometimes you get tired of somebody reminding you that your hometown sucks.

The kid who called T.J. a fag said, "Don't pee your pants, Curtis. I was just kidding," but Curtis is hard to stop once he starts talking. He said, "Well, it's not funny. People can't help it if they're gay and it's not right to hate them and call them fags." Joey Dinwiddie said oh yes it is, because it says in the Bible you shouldn't be gay or you will burn in hell.

Curtis sighed real loud and then he said, "If you are referring to the passage in Leviticus that says homosexuality is a sin, then you also know that gluttony and sloth are sins, too. So that means if you believe gay people are going to burn in hell, everybody who eats like a pig and lives like a slob is going to hell, too. It's going to be a very popular place and a lot of you guys will be there."

McElroy clapped his hands and said, "That's enough," but nobody paid attention to him. He didn't go over and call security, though. He just flopped into his chair and put his head in his hands.

Joey Dinwiddie said, "Yeah, that's enough out of you, Curtis," but Curtis said, "I don't understand why you guys are so interested in other people's sexual preference. It's none of your business—unless you are planning to ask them for a date."

"Because I don't like fags," Joey said. "They make me sick."

95

McElroy stood up but he didn't have to clap his hands and tell us to be quiet because Henry Dominguez stood up, too, and he said, "Shut up," and the way he said "Shut up" made everybody do it. Nobody said anything for a long time and then Henry said, "That's enough," and he sat back down and nobody still said anything because then we all remembered that last year Henry's cousin killed himself after his parents told him they wished he was never born if he was going to be gay.

After Henry's cousin killed himself, a bunch of people wrote letters to the newspaper and said they were sorry to say it but that boy was better off dead. After that, the library put up a little paper on the wall on Gay Pride Week and they put the names of some books you could read if you were gay so you would get some self-esteem and not kill yourself like Henry's cousin did. And the church people made a big protest and now a bunch of church people won't let their kids go to the library anymore which Lupe says is ridiculous.

"They shouldn't be afraid of ideas," Lupe says. "The only people who are afraid of ideas are dumb people who don't know how to think for themselves. Smart people don't believe everything they read. Just because something is in a book doesn't mean it's true."

After McElroy's class, I asked Lupe what did she think about being gay and she said she thinks people are probably gay because of their chromosomes. She's big on biology because she's going to be a doctor. I said, "I don't mean how come people are gay. I mean do you think they are going to hell?" and Lupe said, "I'm not sure there is a hell."

I said, "For reals?" and she said, "I'm not even sure there is a God." When she said that, I crossed myself without even planning to. It was automatic. Lupe laughed and said, "Don't worry, Eddie. If there is a God, he isn't going to kill you for wondering if he exists. He'd be glad that you were using the magnificent brain he gave you. And if there isn't a God, then you don't have to worry about wondering."

I asked Lupe wasn't she Catholic and she said yes and I said then how come she could say those kind of things and she said because she doesn't believe anything unless you can prove it. I said nobody can prove there is a God and she said, "Maybe. Maybe not. I'm researching it."

I laughed because how can you research God, but Lupe said she Googled God on the Internet and he has so many hits it will take her years to read them all. She said some of the Web sites are just stupid but a lot of them are intellectually stimulating. Like she said there are some historians who say that in the original Bible, God was a man and a woman but later on he got changed to just a man. "I ordered a book about it from Amazon.com," Lupe said, "because they wouldn't order it for me at the bookstore here. They said it was blasphemous."

Lupe was impressed that I know what *blasphemous* means, but I learned it last year because a preacher burned a bunch of books right down the street from our house. Before that, I

used to go to church with *mi abuelita* on Sundays because I figured if I got run over by a bus or something sometime and I
hadn't gone to confession, I would still have some good
points in my favor for taking a *vieja* to church. But after that
preacher burned all the books, I stopped going to church because the whole town knew he was going to do it and they
didn't even stop him. He and some of his church friends went
to the store and bought a bunch of Harry Potter and Shakespeare books and burned them up. They didn't even read
them first. They said they didn't have to read them to know
they were full of witchcraft and Satanism. And a whole
bunch of other people went and stood by that book-burning
preacher. They made a holy bonfire. It was in the newspapers
and on TV all over the country, so now Rosablanca is famous
for having crazy book-burners living here.

That book burning made me so mad for two reasons. One,
I know so many little kids who never even owned one book
of their own and if you gave them one they would wrap it up
in a cloth when they weren't reading it so it wouldn't get
dusty. And number two, if you burned even one little corner
of a page of a book in school they would expel you for good.
I know that for a fact because there was this kid named Corey
who lit his math book on fire one day just to show this girl he
would do it and they kicked him out of school so fast and
wouldn't let him come back because he wouldn't tell them
why he did it. They accidentally labeled him an arsonist just
like they accidentally labeled me a sex offender, except they

98

didn't kick me out of school forever. But the school psychologist said Corey was dangerous and they expelled him for good. So when that preacher burned those books, I thought for sure they would kick him out of the church and make him go be one of those warehouse preachers who has like six people in the audience and they are all family. Maybe they would even arrest him. But they didn't arrest him or even yell at him and they didn't kick him out of the church. They just let him keep on going around talking about Jesus like him and Jesus were best friends or something.

That preacher talks too much if you ask me. He should stop talking about going to hell all the time and just go around acting like he is Jesus. Not wearing a white dress and Birkenstocks all the time, but like if he had one of those families in his neighborhood who lives in a falling-down trailer with no electricity and all kinds of junk in the yard, he wouldn't sell his house and move to a nicer neighborhood. He would just go down real quiet to the electric company and pay to have that family's power turned on and he would take them some bags of real delicious food and not just a cardboard box full of canned beans and peas with dust on the top because people had them in the back of their cupboard for ten years before they donated them to the food bank. Or if he saw that crazy lady who sits outside the library with all her stuff in a bag, he would go over and give her a hundred dollars and say a prayer for her and hug her even if she stinks a little bit. And he wouldn't tell anybody he did that stuff. He would just do it nice and quiet. And he would adopt a little orphan from some poor country. Not a movie-star-looking orphan, neither, but a real ugly kid that nobody would want, and he would bring the ugly kid home and feed it good and raise it up right and send it to college so it could be a doctor or a teacher or a judge someday.

And if he saw a gay teenager that nobody liked who always hung out by himself, he wouldn't wish that kid was dead or think about killing him or tell him he is going to burn in hell forever. Even if that gay kid was the preacher's own kid, he wouldn't say he wished the kid had never been born so he would feel like killing himself. He would be nice to that gay kid and he would love that kid even if the kid was against his religion.

I don't know why people have to fight so much about religion and God. You should just be allowed to think what you want and it's nobody's business. Some days I believe in God but some days I don't. Primo says you should pretend you believe in God even if you aren't sure because if you believe in God and you die and there isn't one, then you were just stupid when you were alive. But if you don't believe in God and then you die and there he is, you're in big trouble. I don't think it would do you any good to just pretend to believe in God because if God is so smart he would know you were just faking it. But if you said you were sorry, then he would have to forgive you for faking it because that's not a Ten Commandment. But Primo says no way. If God catches you faking it, he'll get real pissed and you'll be sorry.

Now I know why *mi abuelita* won't let people talk about religion when we're eating except to say a prayer at the beginning because everybody would get indigestion from yelling at each other. Everybody has an opinion about God but nobody can go look it up in the encyclopedia to win the bet and make the other people pay their ten dollars for being so stupid like *mi primo* Enrique always does.

CHAPTER 14

STICK TO THE DEAD DOG

A COUPLE WEEKS AGO, MR. MCELROY WROTE THE WORDS AR-
gument and *fight* on the board and then he drew a line through
fight and said an argument isn't a fight with a winner and a
loser, it's just people exchanging ideas—which is exactly the
kind of thing that teachers say and you wonder if they can
hear how stupid they sound and do they really believe all that
crap. I never heard anybody have an argument where they ex-
change ideas like old baseball cards. If it's my uncles, they
start out trading jokes and then insults and then punches. If
it's me and Papi, we skip the jokes and the insults.

McElroy made us read this whole article about how to argue the right way, like you have to stick to the topic of your
argument the whole way. You can't bring in all the stuff

you've been saving up to nuke the other guy with. So, if some dickhead got drunk and ran over your dog, you had to just say how sad you were to lose your pup and not bring up the fact that the same guy borrowed your lawn mower and brought it back with a broken starter or came over your house to watch the Super Bowl and drank seventeen beers and then never even invited you over his house to watch his new plasma TV.

You have to just stick to that dead dog. And you can't do all the normal argument stuff like call the other person names, or break some dishes, or scream your guts out, or take off and don't come back until tomorrow, or turn up the stereo so loud you can't hear the other person and you both get brain damage. You can't even do little shit like say the other guy is a liar and a freaking loser who can't even afford his own lawn mower. You have to say everything from your point of view, like instead of saying, "You're a selfish dickhead for borrowing my shit and bringing it back broken," you have to say, "I feel like you don't value my friendship or respect my property."

I totally forgot all about that argument crap until Lupe got so mad she almost broke up with me. It's not like we never had a fight before, but usually we just have those little kinds that you can get over pretty fast if you go out and eat some good green chile enchiladas in a dark place that has a little candle on the table so you look real handsome, or if you rent a movie and sit on opposite ends of the couch with the soles of your bare feet touching each other for the whole thing even if you feel like grabbing each other's *nalgas* halfway through.

But this time nothing worked even though the whole thing seemed pretty lame to me. Lupe got so mad just because me and her have a whole different idea about time. We got different kinds of clocks ticking in our heads. Like she thinks *a little while* means two minutes or even two seconds, and I think *a little while* depends on what I'm doing right now. Like if I'm changing the oil in Papi's truck, a little while is probably thirty minutes. If I'm taking a shower, it could be anywhere from two minutes to twenty minutes, depending on certain things.

Anyway, Lupe called me last Wednesday night and asked me did I want to walk down to Caliche's and get a frozen custard with her because she needed some chocolate custard with chocolate sauce and chocolate chips or she would lose her mind because of some hormone imbalance that I didn't want to hear the details about, so I told her to hold on and I would be over her house in a little while. I hurried up and finished my chores but I had a lot of extra work on account of I sneaked out the night before to help Henry Dominguez steal his little brother's bicycle back from the creep who stole it and Papi caught me coming back in at 3 a.m. He didn't hit me or yell at me, but he didn't argue good, neither. He just shook his head and went back in him and Mami's room and shut the door real quiet. In the morning, Mami looked at me real sad and told me all the extra chores Papi put on my list.

By the time I got done with everything, it was about two hours until I got over to Lupe's and by the time we got to Caliche's, they just turned over the CLOSED sign. Lupe stood there staring at the door, looking so sad that I thought maybe the owner lady who was standing inside would feel sorry for her and open up for five more minutes, but she didn't. For a couple seconds Lupe looked like she was going to cry. Then she looked like she just stepped on a goat head in her bare feet. Then she looked at me real hard and closed her eyes and sat down on this little cement bench and hugged herself with both arms and just stared at her knees. When I sat down and put my arm around her, she just about knocked me off the bench and said, "Leave me alone," and she meant it.

I didn't try to put my arm around her again, but I sat back down and said, "I'm real sorry, Lupe, but I had a good reason for being late."

"You always have a reason," Lupe hollered. "You're always late and you always have a reason. But you're the only one who thinks they're good reasons. I think they suck!"

I whispered that maybe she shouldn't holler so loud, but she hollered even louder, "What's the matter? Don't you want anybody to know that you're too dumb to tell time? And you don't even care enough about me to look at your watch?"

I was thinking to holler back that why would I look at my watch if I was too dumb to tell time, and just because she had cramps didn't mean she had to act like a you-know-what, and if she wasn't such a spoiled little daddy's girl, she wouldn't expect everybody to do what she wanted every single second, but right before I started yelling, I remembered that argument article which is probably the only reason that Lupe and me are still together. Instead of saying all that mean stuff, I said real quiet, "I'm sorry I disappointed you by being late today. I'm sorry that you have cramps. And I will try to be on time in the future because . . . *yo te quiero.*"

I actually said it. I had thought it a bunch of times but I never told Lupe before that I loved her. Then I just shut up and waited like the article said, to give the other person a turn.

Lupe didn't say anything for a long time. She just sat there with her lips pooched out like a mad baby, and she breathed real noisy a couple times, and then she started crying.

"You love me?" she said and I said, "Yeah," and she said, "Me too," and then she stopped sniffling and we decided that we would stop saying things like "a little while" or "later on" and we would say an exact time like 2:15 or 3:45 and if I was going to be more than ten minutes late, I would call her cell phone.

For a couple seconds I felt the same as when my mom says I have to call if I'm not going to be home by a certain time, like how come people have to try to tie you up like a dog or treat you like a baby. Then Lupe scooted over on the bench and put her hand on my leg and touched it real soft up and down with her fingertips. And she leaned her head on my shoulder and I could smell her hair which really does smell like an angel, and I didn't care if I had to call her every minute for the rest of my life because if something doesn't really hurt you but it makes somebody you care about real happy, you should just go ahead and do it.

That's the kind of stuff they should be teaching us in school. It's okay to learn algebra and biology and grammar and all that stuff, but you could always learn that stuff from a book all by yourself. They should teach us the stuff we really need to learn—like how to make somebody really love you, and how to turn off that little voice in your head that tells you what a loser you are, and how to teach your dog to pee where it's supposed to, and how to get over being sad when your little cousin dies, and how to talk to your father without both of you getting so mad. But they probably couldn't teach us stuff like that in school even if they wanted to, because if they teach something in school they have to give you a test to make sure how much you learned.

They need to stop giving so many tests in school because they're making everybody hate school, even the kids who used to like it. If they have to give so many tests, at least they could give the kind where you have to make up your own answer and not just guess which one is right. Primo says a monkey could pass a multiple choice test fifty percent of the time and he's probably right because one time T.J. Ritchie got everybody in our math class to put down all C's or else all B's for the test and then take a little nap for the rest of the test period. T.J. got busted for being the mastermind of the whole thing but they didn't expel him because the kids who put all C's passed the test, including me. In fact, that was one of my best math grades ever which was probably pretty embarrassing for the math teacher who made up that test.

"They got the whole thing backasswards," T.J. said when we were sitting outside the principal's office waiting for his mother, who was inside promising to take him straight to church to talk to the preacher when they got home. I didn't have to be at the office but I was sitting there anyways. Sometimes I sit there because the secretaries don't bother you. They think you're sitting there waiting to get yelled at, not just sitting there because even staring at a blank wall is way more interesting than math class.

"They keep giving all these tests because half the kids in New Mexico flunk out of school because they can't read or do fractions," T.J. said. "But they keep teaching the same stupid shit. That's why they keep getting the same stupid test scores."

He grabbed my notebook and drew a picture of a dog. He drew a giant pile of steamy crap behind the dog's tail and a big bowl in front of its head that was filled with schoolbooks. T.J. draws real good, almost as good as Primo who could probably have been a professional artist but he flunked out of art class because the teacher said he had to draw pictures of a chair and a vase and a bowl of oranges instead of lowriders and couples dancing the tango and sexy girls with tattoos on their *nalgas*.

"You keep feeding the dog the same crap," T.J. said, "you get the same shit. You can test that shit and test that shit and test that shit and it's still going to stink because *mierda* is *mierda*."

T.J. grinned at me like a maniac for a second and then kept on drawing dog shit until the whole page was covered with it. Then he handed me my notebook and stood up and walked right out the front door of the school even though his mother was still inside talking. None of the secretaries said anything. They just watched him go out the door and down the sidewalk and across the street. He kept right on walking until he finally disappeared.

CHAPTER 15

WHO IS EDDIE CORAZON?

Lupe's father has eyes like a bullfighter, real shiny and hard, so you know he could just stand there until the very last second and then stick a knife in your neck right when you thought you were winning. No wonder Lupe is so strong, with a father like that. The first time I met Mr. Garcia, he didn't look at me with hard eyes because he didn't hate me yet. But he looked me over real good so I would know I would only get one chance with him so I better not mess it up. But I did. I messed it up big. Now Lupe isn't even allowed to talk to me because I'm a negative influence over her. I'm probably the most negative influence she ever had because nobody else ever made her get arrested before.

If we still had sex ed in school like they used to, probably the whole thing wouldn't have even happened. Primo says they used to teach stuff that you could do besides you-know-what so nobody would get pregnant or get a disease, and they used to give out free condoms, too. But now we just have abstinence, so everybody just does what comes naturally. I was willing to take my chances but Lupe wasn't and it was making me *loco* until Jaime and his girlfriend took too many chances. Then I was glad that Lupe is the boss of us sometimes and makes me listen to her or else.

Jaime bought some birth control pills from T.J. Ritchie, except they turned out to be baby aspirins. Lena freaked out and said they had to go to Planned Parenthood right away but Jaime doesn't have a driver's license. His father took it away after Jaime got busted trying to get into a nightclub in El Paso with his father's ID. So Jaime asked me would I take him. Papi already took away my car and sold it and gave me that stupid bicycle that I never ride, so I told Papi I had a job interview right after school and he let me borrow his car. Jaime said to just let him take the car, but I'm not that stupid. I didn't really want to go because I stopped cutting classes and I been trying to bring up my grades so Lupe won't be ashamed of having a dumb boyfriend. But Jaime and me have been friends since first grade and he always has my back, so I had to help him out. We made a plan to cut out right before lunch so we could be back in time for sixth period.

I knew I shouldn't have let Lupe come with us but my brain isn't my biggest body part when she's around, if you know what I mean. When Lupe found out about the plan, she said she was going, too, because Lena needed another girl to sit with her. I said no, and she said yes, and I said no, and Lupe put her hands on her hips and I gave up because when a woman puts her hands on her hips, if you don't give her what she wants, you'll be sorry.

Everything would have been just fine because Lena wasn't pregnant, but I got filled with lust and let Jaime drive back to school so I could sit in the backseat with Lupe. Lena wasn't in the mood to even talk to Jaime, so I figured why waste the backseat on two people who didn't even want to hold hands. Lena cried all the way back to school and it made Jaime so nervous that he crashed the car. We almost made it, but he drove right into the back of a big black SUV about two blocks from school. This old Anglo guy was driving, so you know he has insurance and he quick called the cops. If it would have been a Mexican car, we could have probably just gave the guy some money because *mi primo* Octavio can do any kind of bodywork you need and you can't even tell the car was crashed after he gets done.

Mr. Garcia got there even before the police and as soon as he saw nobody got hurt, he said, "Eduardo, why don't we take a little walk?" It wasn't a real question because he already had his arm around my shoulder. We walked about fifty feet and then Mr. Garcia stopped and said, "Look at my daughter." Lupe was still standing by the smashed-up cars talking to the police who was Sgt. Cabrera, that lady cop who came to

Beecher's class and I had to be the escort. When the cop car pulled up and I saw who was driving, I was hoping Sgt. Cabrera wouldn't remember me, but as soon as she got out of the car, she said, "Yo, Eddie. How'd you like that book?"

After I escorted her, Sgt. Cabrera sent me that book she was talking about, *The Four Agreements*, except I never read it. I just put it in the back of the little drawer where I keep my socks and forgot about it, but I told her it was real good and thanks for sending it to me.

Sgt. Cabrera shook her head but she didn't call me a liar. Instead, she said, "You don't read that book here," and she pointed to her head. "You read it here." She put her hand on her heart like saying the Pledge of Allegiance. Then she stopped being friendly because she had to arrest me and call my parents.

I was glad Mr. Garcia got there first because other people's parents never yell at you as loud as your own parents do. When I saw his face, I thought Mr. Garcia might punch me, but instead he said let's take a little walk, so we did. "Look at my beautiful daughter," he said again. We both looked at Lupe. I nodded because I couldn't say anything because Lupe is so beautiful it can make you cry.

"She's not just beautiful," Mr. Garcia said. "She's gifted and talented and she is going to make something big out of her life." Usually it's the mothers who say that kind of stuff and usually you think, Yeah, right, keep dreaming, lady, but Mr. Garcia wasn't dreaming. Lupe is so smart and *hermosa*

113

that she sparkles and her father is so proud he shines from it, and I am the kind of kid who is so stupid he makes his father almost get a heart attack and makes his mother cross herself and whisper *"Madre de Dios"* about twenty times a day.

"Lupe deserves a man she can respect," Mr. Garcia said, "a man I can respect," and he poked his finger into his chest which must be pretty hard because it sounded like he was knocking on wood. So when Mr. Garcia said he thought it would be a good idea if Lupe didn't see me for a while except in school, I didn't argue with him. Besides, I knew I would probably be grounded forever anyways after Papi got there.

Me and Mr. Garcia were still about twenty feet away but I could hear Papi yelling on the phone when Sgt. Cabrera called him. I was thinking how embarrassed I would be when he showed up and started yelling at me in front of everybody, but he didn't even yell. He rode up on that stupid bicycle he bought me after he took away my car and just got off the bike and let it fall on the ground. Then he snapped his fingers at me and pointed to the bike so I knew I wasn't riding home in his car.

When I finally got home, my gym bag and a little suitcase were sitting on the front porch outside the door. I figured out pretty quick that Papi was kicking me out because he warned me a lot of times that one of these days I was going to say I was sorry but he was going to say, "Sorry doesn't live here anymore."

Mami hardly ever yells, even when Papi does, but she

talks loud and I could hear her before I even got to the door. I could hear them both. Mami said, "Give him a chance," and Papi said, "That's the problem, *querida*. You give him so many chances and he keeps blowing them. He's never going to act like a man if you treat him like a baby." Mami said something I couldn't hear too good, but I heard her say Lupe's name and Papi yelled, "If she's so smart, what's she doing with a *menso* who keeps flunking biology?" Then he started swearing in Spanish, so I coughed and made some noises and went in the house.

Papi crossed his arms and stared at me from across the kitchen. Mami started to come over and hug me, but he made a noise in his throat and she stopped and went over and sat down at the table. I told Papi I didn't even care if he grounded me forever or kicked me out of the house because it didn't matter anyway since Mr. Garcia said Lupe couldn't go out with me anymore. She can't even call me on the phone because I'm such a negative influence and a loser.

Papi said Mr. Garcia is pretty smart because him and Papi are thinking down the same road. He said Jaime and Primo are negative influences over me so he's sending me to Truth or Consequences to stay with his brother, *mi tío* Antonio, until school gets out for the summer. Of all my uncles, I like Tío Antonio the most even though I don't know him that good. He's a park ranger and a bachelor and he is totally buff and he's going to whip my *nalgas* into shape. I hope he does it, too, because then maybe Lupe and Papi and everybody can stop

115

being ashamed of me and start being proud of me for a change.

I been to T or C a lot of times to visit, so it's not like I'm going someplace where I don't know my way around. I got a lot of older cousins over there, like *mi primo* Miguel who graduated high school and went to TVI in Albuquerque and got a real good job as a X-ray technician at a hospital, which is the first time my mother tried to make me promise that I would start setting a good example for *los niños* and graduate high school because I'm way smarter than Miguel. So anyways, I been to T or C a lot and the last time I was there, I found this bookstore called the Black Cat downtown near the skate park. It's a little bookstore, not like Barnes & Noble or Hastings where if a guy who looks like me goes there right away the detective starts following him around waiting for him to steal something.

The Black Cat doesn't even have a detective, just this one lady with long yellow hair and a green hat. Not a church hat. Just a hat for fun. When I walked in, she didn't even look nervous like I might steal something. She just said, "Hello," and kept on petting her cat who sneaked down and ate my shoelaces when I was busy looking at the books. The lady even offered to buy me some new laces but it wasn't her fault and besides it made me feel kind of special for a cat to eat my shoelaces, so I told her never mind.

It was a Saturday when I went to the bookstore and the lady told me if I come back the next day there will be a poetry reading. She said I could hear some of the local poets do their thing but Papi likes to hit the road early in the morning whenever we visit someplace so I didn't get to go. I didn't really want to go to the poetry reading back then because that was before I wrote my poems and I still thought poems were all boring like the ones in school. Now I think maybe it would be kind of interesting.

There's a lot of things I used to think I wouldn't like but it turned out I do, like ballroom dancing and writing poetry. *Mi primo* Enrique says I better watch out or else I'm going to turn into a intellectual and then I'll get my ass kicked all the time. I said what about Harvey Castro. He's the smartest kid in his school and nobody kicks his ass. Primo said yeah, but you're not Harvey Castro, you're Eddie Corazon. And I said, "Who is Eddie Corazon?" but Primo thought I was making a joke, so he just laughed. But it wasn't a joke. It was a real question except I don't know the answer.

CHAPTER 16

MAKING BABIES

When me and Jaime were sitting in the car outside Planned Parenthood waiting to find out if Lena was pregnant, Jaime was too nervous to have a conversation, so we just sat there and stared at the sky and the dirt with all the weeds and cactuses. And I started thinking that it isn't such a good plan the way people have babies all the time whether they want them or not. I thought what if instead of having sex to make babies, people just had sex for fun and babies got made the same way yucca plants make a new baby yucca when they die. When the yucca gets real old, it kind of leans over and instead of sticking a big stalk with flowers straight up into the air, the stalk goes out sideways and plants its top into the ground. Pretty soon there's a new little yucca growing out of

118

that old stalk and the old yucca hangs around for a while and then it just dries up and gets blown away unless some cow or deer who can't find anything good to eat comes by and chomps it up. It's like a whole big circle from living to dying, right there in the desert.

So, instead of making so many babies and filling up the world with so much population that people are starving all over the place, every person would just make one new baby when they died. And if people just dried up and disappeared after a while, you could save a bunch of money on funerals and stuff and you wouldn't have to hurry up and go see them before they start to stink. You could just take your time as long as you got there before they got too dried up and blown away.

After the new baby got sprouted, all the other alive people would have to take care of the baby, so if somebody sucked or was a child molester or something, the other people would just pull up that person's new little baby plant before it got ripe and they'd ditch it. You wouldn't have too much population growth that way, but I guess eventually you wouldn't have enough people because some of them would get chomped by a cow.

But I think it could still be a good idea if I figured it out better. I could probably figure it out real perfect if I used the plan Beecher showed us for how to solve a problem. Too bad she didn't use that plan to figure out how to not get fired for being a liberal intellectual. Anyway, if you have a problem, you shouldn't just do the first thing that pops into your head because what if you just had a candy bar for lunch so your brain wasn't working too good, or you snitched a bottle of tequila from your *abuelita*'s kitchen the night before and you woke up temporarily stupid. Instead of jumping on the first idea you think of, you're supposed to use this special formula, like you have to identify your problem and brainstorm solutions and figure out if one of them would really work. Beecher gave us some sample problems to work on in groups.

Sometimes I like group work, but not if I get stuck with T.J. Ritchie who just leans back and crosses his arms and laughs at you and calls you kiss-ass pussies if you try to do the work, even if it's kind of interesting. I got in a good problem group that day, though, with a couple of Anglo girls who wear glasses and no makeup so you can tell they want you to admire their brains instead of their *chichis*. Our example problem was what should you do if you have a teacher who hates you for real and it's not just your imagination. I was pretty surprised when those smart girls brainstormed all kinds of torture we could do to the teacher, which was pretty fun. But then when we had to choose a real solution that you wouldn't go to jail for, we came up with some pretty good ideas, like when that teacher calls you "beaner brain" or tells you that you're a worthless piece of shit, you could secretly record it on your cell phone and then put it on YouTube so they couldn't say you were a psycho liar who needs to get on medication before you crack up and bring an AK-47 to school.

Henry Dominguez's group got a good problem, too, about what if a couple of stupid kids keep disrupting your class, so the teacher makes a real stupid seating chart where you don't get to sit by anybody good and maybe you even have to sit right next to the teacher's desk or beside some kid who picks his nose and wipes it on his pants all day long. Henry's group solved the seating problem and came up with a plan that was so good that Beecher actually used it. The plan was: Some kids need to sit in the same seats every day or else they freak out, so they get to claim a seat and it's their seat even if they are absent. Other kids get bored from sitting in the same seat beside the same people every day, so they get to choose a new seat every day from the ones that are left. But nobody gets to sit in the back if they have a bad grade because then they cause too much trouble and everybody has to listen to their same old shit all the time. So, if you have a D or a F, you have to sit in the front two rows. That makes those losers work a little bit harder so they can get away from the teacher. It's a pretty good plan and I like it because I get to sit in the back corner, which is my favorite because I'm like *mi primo* Enrique when it comes to sitting in a place with a lot of other people. We like to sit with our back against the wall so we don't have to worry who's behind us and what they could be thinking to do.

Jaime's group got this totally lame problem of what should you do if your favorite teacher has bad breath which is a totally stupid problem because teachers went to college so they should be smart enough to notice if all the kids are leaning way back whenever that teacher talks to them, and even though teacher pay is pretty crappy, they could at least buy some peppermint gum or some Tic Tacs if they couldn't afford some new teeth.

I tried to think of how I could use that problem plan to get rid of my current situation but my problems are too big. Even if I could figure out how to make Papi not be so mad about me lying to him and wrecking his car, I would still have the little problem of cutting school and making up the assignments, plus the real big problem of Lupe's father. Mr. Garcia is not the kind of guy you could brainstorm any good solutions about how to handle him because he knows how to brainstorm back at you. Like when they go to court, one of the lawyers brainstorms how to stick somebody in jail and the other lawyer brainstorms how to keep the guy out of jail or get a deal. All the lawyers are smart enough to graduate college and they got all kind of tricks up the sleeve of their three-piece suits, but Mr. Garcia always wins.

Lupe told me she had to work real hard to come up with an argument for why she should be allowed to transfer to Bright Horizons because Mr. Garcia didn't want her to go to an alternative school. He wanted to just sue Cheyenne for beating up Lupe all the time at the regular high school, or else sue the school for suspending Lupe because of being involved in a violent altercation. But Lupe didn't want to sue anybody. So she made up a case, like she was going to court, with statistics that show how many kids graduate from Bright Horizons and how many of them go to college, and how come it wouldn't be right to sue either Cheyenne who is retarded or the school district because they don't even have enough money for computers in the library.

"I only won my case fifty percent," Lupe said. "Daddy only agreed that I could go to Bright Horizons for one semester and then he would evaluate the situation. But with Daddy, fifty percent is pretty good."

If Lupe can only win fifty percent and Mr. Garcia loves her so much, then I figure my chances aren't too good. But I'm not giving up. I'll just keep my nose clean and keep brainstorming.

CHAPTER 17

THE FOUR AGREEMENTS

I BEEN THINKING THAT SINCE NOBODY KNOWS ME VERY GOOD in Truth or Consequences, I could maybe change a little bit. Like I could shave my three chin hairs which probably don't look as cool as I thought they did. And I could tuck in my shirt and not wear a bandanna and be a intellectual. I could be Eduardo instead of Eddie and start out getting good grades, so right away I would be lumped with the kiss-ass kids instead of with the losers. I would probably get beat up a little bit, but I can handle it. Besides, after I graduate, I can be as smart as I want to because after you get out of school people don't beat you up for being smart. They give you money instead.

It's a good thing I'm just in a gang with *mis primos* in Rosablanca and not with a real gang because I couldn't just decide to quit hanging with a real gang, I would have to get jumped out and maybe even killed. Jaime's brother Xavier tried to get out of the 10th Street Posse and they beat him down so bad they broke all his teeth and they told him if he went back to school they would kill him, so he had to go get a GED instead. Xavier wanted to get out of the Posse because his girlfriend had a baby and Xavier wanted to be a regular dad and not a gangbanger whose kids would probably be little bangers. I used to think I needed the gang so the drug dealers wouldn't try to make me be their go-boy because I would never be walking by myself where they could get me. But after I met Lupe, I started hanging around with her most of the time, and I started thinking about my future just like Xavier. If they heard me say it, they would kill me for sure but I think maybe if the real gangbangers had somebody to love them real good they wouldn't need to be in a gang. Even if your mother loves you, maybe it isn't enough, because your mother isn't out there on the streets where you have to deal with all kinds of shit. Maybe you need somebody your own age who can look you eye to eye and see you for real and still love you anyways and that person tells you to stop acting like a loser and get some goals for your future. Then you don't need a gang or even a bunch of homies to hang with because you don't feel alone and you are going someplace.

These are my new thoughts that I am creating so I can have a new reality where I'm not a loser and a negative influence over Lupe. I got these new thoughts from reading that book Sgt. Cabrera gave me. If I wouldn't have read that book, I wouldn't have decided to be a intellectual because I had two other plans. One was to go out and get a gun and get real drunk and steal a car and drive around with the gun on the dashboard so when the cops pulled me over, I would reach for the gun and they would shoot me dead. That wasn't too good of a plan because then Lupe would be sad forever and what if the cop was Sgt. Cabrera who would feel real bad for killing a kid she gave a book to. My other plan was to take off with Enrique and go to Mexico except there aren't hardly any good jobs there which is why so many people come here and pick chiles for about two cents an hour.

But after I read *The Four Agreements*, I gave up those plans which turned out to be a real good thing. I wasn't even going to read that book because I looked it over a little bit back when Sgt. Cabrera first gave it to me and it looked pretty lame. It's a real skinny book with hardly any big words. You're just supposed to do four things and your life will change: Always do your best. Don't take anything personally. Never make assumptions and be impeccable with your word. That's the kind of stuff they teach you in kindergarten or first grade, except little kids don't know what *assumption* or *impeccable* means so the teachers just say, "Don't go around thinking you know everything and don't tell lies and if somebody calls you a bad name, they're the stupid one." So it didn't seem like a book you would give to somebody and then act like it was a real big deal.

But I had a lot of time on my hands. After I got arrested,

Papi took my cell phone, so I can't even text anybody, and he canceled the Internet, so no e-mail, neither. For a couple days I had electronics withdrawal. My ears felt so empty that it made a loud echo inside my head and I was wishing that I could go someplace to get away from myself. If I wasn't a secret reader, I probably would of lost it like Jaime's neighbor who married a church girl and then tried to quit drinking and smoking and watching porn all at the same time and it freaked him out so bad he drank some Drano and had to get locked up for his own good. But whenever I felt like I was losing it, I would just read a book.

After I read all the books in the house, I was packing up my stuff to take over to Tío's and I found *The Four Agreements* under my socks. I figured I might as well read it because even though Sgt. Cabrera was a cop, she was kind of cool and you could tell from looking in her eyes that she was still hanging in there. Sometimes if you look at old people, even if they aren't drunk or stoned, they have this look in their eyes like it's all over so who cares. Maybe they wish they never got married or why did they have that last kid or why couldn't they have normal kids instead of the ones they got and how come they let their wife make them sell their motorcycle, or they could be thinking that it's all just a big rip-off because even if you live your life real clean and work hard and save your money and go to church every week and never beat your kids or have adultery, you could still end up with a life that sucks.

As soon as I read that book, I could see why Sgt. Cabrera

said you have to read it with your heart and not your head because it sounds too simple to give you any good advice unless you take it to the next level. Like instead of just not telling lies to other people, you shouldn't tell lies to yourself, neither. Like if you really care about graduating high school then don't tell yourself you don't care and flunk all your classes and then wonder why you're such a loser.

Before, I didn't get it when Sgt. Cabrera said your thoughts create your reality. That sounds like one of those feeling-good posters they hang on the wall that nobody reads. But this time, I got it. The light turned on in my brain and it was shining so bright that I could see all my lame ideas just sitting in there looking at me with a stupid expression on their face. Like I saw that thought which was *How long could a girl like Lupe love a loser like me?* And I knew if I kept that thought in my head, Lupe would stop loving me and I would be a loser for real and end up in jail or something.

I used to didn't get the connection because I skipped the middle part about intentions. I was thinking that your thoughts can't create reality because if that worked then all those losers who think they are going to be NBA superstars or rap masters someday would actually be those things. You can't just think stuff and create a reality, you have to think of an intention to make something happen. Like you can just go around thinking how much you hate school and you still won't be a juvenile delinquent unless you make an intention to get in trouble like I did, so I ended up at the alt school. And I created the intention to get a girlfriend, so I joined ballroom dance and got Lupe and now we got our own reality. Then I created the stupid intention to lie to Papi about his car and I created everybody getting arrested.

So I kicked all the old thoughts out of my head to make room for a bunch of new ones with good intentions attached to them. Now I don't even think of letting go of Lupe or being a loser. Instead, I am creating the thought of being a success and making the intention to graduate and get a good job and maybe even go to college so I can be the kind of man who can look Lupe's father straight in the eye for as long as it takes.

The reason I'm thinking on maybe going to college is this dude from New Mexico State came to McElroy's class to inspire us to go to college and he was a professor even though he was Mexican and had a mustache and a ponytail. After he got done inspiring us and everybody was fooling around, I asked that professor what if somebody's grades were real good for a few years and then real bad for some more years and then real good right at the end. He said as long as your senior year is real good, you can probably go to NMSU if you graduate and get some good recommendations from your teachers. McElroy might give me a good recommendation because he would be happy that he was a good influence and I didn't drop out of school, but I don't want to ask him. He probably doesn't even know all the stuff I been thinking, but it's not right to ask somebody to do you a favor after you been going around thinking they are a stupid *pinche* dickhead.

Beecher would probably give me a recommendation if I asked her unless she already forgot who I am. She's still working at the library so I guess she didn't go teach those Indian kids like I thought she would. She probably wants to wait until next year so she can start fresh instead of taking over for some crappy teacher that got fired or just quit because it was too hard trying to motivate people like me and Henry Dominguez and T.J. Ritchie.

At first, I was thinking that maybe I would check out some library books sometime when Beecher wasn't working and then the next time I went to pick up Letty and Juanito from story hour I would put the books in that book drop and I would put my journal in there, too. If some other library lady got it, she would probably just throw my journal away since it doesn't have my name on it or anything. But if Beecher got it, she might recognize how I write. She might even remember some of the other stuff I wrote. Like this one essay she gave me extra credit for having a sense of humor. Beecher would give you a better grade for having a sense of humor even if you used a swearword or bad spelling because she liked us to have our own ideas.

"You can always correct the spelling and grammar in an interesting essay," Beecher used to tell us, "but if your essay is perfect and boring, then it's perfectly boring." Before they killed Saddam Hussein, Beecher asked us to write in our journal what we thought Saddam would be like if he was a kid in our class at Bright Horizons. And here's what I wrote:

130

Well, let me tell you. If Saddam Hussein was a kid in this class today we wouldn't have all this war stuff and a lot of people wouldn't be dying. Also if he was a kid in this class we wouldn't make all those diaper on your head jokes because we aren't allowed to hurt people's feelings. Saddam would probably have a dad who owned a Pic Quik and he would get all the sodas he wanted. Or else his dad might own a gas station and he would get free gas so everybody would be his friend. And if he was in this class today, I think Saddam would probably wear some cheap plastic shoes and those polyester slacks with a plaid button-up shirt and once in a while he would wear some bell-bottoms. Or else he would wear camouflage clothes because he likes to look like he's in the army. He would probably wear sideburns because he would think they were cool except he wouldn't comb his hair or brush his teeth and never clean his ears so he would have real yellow teeth and his ears would be full of that earwax junk. Probably his feet would smell like Nacho Cheese Doritos. Nobody would want to sit next to him and then Miss Beecher would say, "Everybody sit in the first four rows except Saddam you can sit in the back." If somebody did sit behind him they would stick him with their pencil.

Saddam would have terrible social skills. He
would steal people's lunch money and he would
always write dirty stuff on the desks so even Miss
Beecher wouldn't like him. When nobody was
looking, she would hit him in the head. For sure,
Saddam would always want to copy off everybody
but nobody would let him copy their papers
because he's a punk-ass trick. And if he ever tried
to mess with me, I would beat his ass.

Beecher gave me a good grade on that journal and she wrote on the side of the paper, "Watch out for stereotypes, but thank you for making me smile, Eddie," so maybe she would remember that smile. But it could be that she forgot all about me as soon as she stopped being my teacher. Just because you remember somebody real good doesn't mean they remember you back.

Before, I was thinking I would put my journal in the library drop box so Beecher could read all those serious pages that I wrote and never turned in for a grade because I didn't want her to know too much personal stuff about me. And I'd put one of my poems on the last page. But my new intention is different. Instead of putting it in the drop box, I will walk right up and hand my journal to Beecher and if she says, "What's this?" I'll say, "I'm Eddie Corazon in case you forgot me and that's my journal that I wrote when you were our teacher but I never gave it to you." And then I'll say, "I just

132

want you to know that even if you were only there for a couple of months, you were still the best teacher I ever had." And then I will probably start feeling weird and I will feel like running right out of the library but I won't run. I will stand right there and wait.

CHAPTER 18

PLAN C: ALKA-SELTZER IN YOUR POCKET

It's working. I'm creating my new reality in Truth or Consequences. Everybody calls me Eduardo and I sit with the brains and brownies at school. I wasn't sure I would like being a intellectual as much as being a juvenile delinquent but then I had to think about it with an impeccable attitude. I asked myself straight up which was better and I had to admit it's easier just letting your brain breathe like it wants to instead of always thinking about how you have to be so cool and look ruthless and walk dangerous and pretend you can't hardly even read.

Tío Antonio moved since the last time we visited him. Instead of living in T or C, now he lives in a little brown house at the end of this little park down along the Rio

Grande that is part of Elephant Butte State Park. It's way different from living in a town. Mostly it is just trees and cactuses and a lot of ducks. There are about ten little adobe *casitas* where people can camp and a walking trail that goes all along the river so you can stop and fish or have a picnic. There isn't any school out there, so I ride the bus to T or C which has a brand-new high school that looks a lot better than most schools in New Mexico which usually have so much graffiti and broken stuff they look like Pancho Villa used to hide out there.

The first day, this one kid, Francisco, started dogging me. I wasn't too surprised because when the teacher asked me what was my name and I was thinking whether to say "Eddie" or "Eduardo," I saw him watching real close, like if I said the wrong thing I was history. But if you back down from your plans every time some loser dogs you, you'll never get anyplace, so I stuck with my agenda and figured Francisco would either chill out or I'd have to deal with him later.

I was expecting some kind of trouble, because I figured being a intellectual wouldn't be as easy as all the teachers think. So I had some backup plans just in case Plan A: Thinking Like a Intellectual didn't work out. Plan B was Get Glasses because a lot of guys won't hit you if you're wearing glasses. Since I got twenty-twenty vision, I couldn't get glasses from a doctor, so I tried on those cheap glasses for old people that they sell at Pic Quik. Those glasses made everything too blurry, and besides, they were real ugly and I'd rather fight than look that stupid. So I decided to make some fake glasses like this one guy wore in the movie *Blue in the Face* that Beecher tried to show us once before she knew better.

Beecher said she was trying to introduce us to a different kind of movie with no car crashes in it, but then we got to the scene where the sexy jealous girlfriend comes into the smoke shop wearing a red suit and she takes off her jacket and she's just wearing a lacy black bra and you could see the top of her black thong because her skirt was real low and tight. She grabs her boyfriend by the pants and says, "I'm going to ride you like a bull," and all the guys started cheering and some of the girls screamed.

Somebody must of been passing by our room and snitched because a couple minutes later the principal came in and called Miss Beecher out into the hall. We didn't get to watch the rest of the movie in class, but me and Jaime asked Primo to check it out from the video store and we watched the whole thing twice. It was pretty good for an old-people kind of movie with no excitement in it except sex. And there was this one guy working in a store who wore glasses that were real glasses with no glass. They looked like regular glasses unless you looked real close.

Just in case Plan B didn't work, I made a second backup plan, Plan C: Keep an Alka-Seltzer in Your Pocket. Plan C turned out to be the one that worked.

After school, I went to the library on my way to the bus

loading zone and when I came out of the library, Francisco was leaning against the wall, smoking. He kept his cigarette all curled up inside his hand and he blew the smoke out real slow so that you couldn't see it from very far away, so I figured he wasn't as bad as he liked people to think he was or else he wouldn't be so worried about getting busted.

When I saw Francisco standing there, waiting for me, at first I started thinking could I take him or should I throw the first punch or wait for him, but then I remembered to think like a intellectual, like Harvey Castro who never fights. And I thought, What would Harvey Castro do? and I thought Harvey Castro wouldn't even think about fighting. He wouldn't even let that intention into his head as Plan B. He'd just go right on walking around being intellectual and not getting into fights no matter what people said.

"Wassup?" I said to Francisco, and I didn't even shift my books so I'd be in a good position to throw a punch. He didn't say anything, but when I got close to him, he stepped out and bumped me hard with his shoulder. I just stopped and looked at him, but not with a fighting expression on my face. I was wearing my fake glasses, but I knew they weren't going to be much help because you could tell Francisco was the kind of kid who would punch you in the glasses and break them right on your face.

"Where you from?" he said, and I said, "Rosablanca," and he said, "What you doing over here?"

I thought about saying something smart, but Harvey

Castro would probably tell the truth, so I said, "Staying with *mi tío* Antonio until the end of the school year and trying to turn over a new leaf and stop getting in so much trouble so my girlfriend's father will stop thinking I'm such a bad influence."

Francisco's face wrinkled up a little bit around his eyes and I thought he might smile, but he didn't. He threw his cigarette on the ground and smashed it with his boot. He was wearing Ropers which isn't a good sign in a fight because they hurt a lot worse than tennis shoes if you get kicked, especially you-know-where.

"Well, I have to go or I'll miss my bus," I said, and I tried to walk past, but Francisco stuck his arm out so I ran into it. I decided that if I lived long enough to get back to Rosablanca I would ask Harvey Castro where I could sign up for some kung fu. I dropped my books on the ground and stepped back to get a good take on Francisco before I remembered Plan C. Francisco wasn't moving yet, so I decided to give it a try. I turned around partways so he couldn't see my face and I took the Alka-Seltzer out of my pocket and slipped it into my mouth. The plan was for it to start foaming and then I would look like a lunatic and nobody would want to fight me. But it didn't foam. It just sat on my tongue, sizzling a little bit, and tickling my whole mouth.

Francisco drew back and I ducked and when I did, that Alka-Seltzer jumped back into my throat and made me choke. It was stuck to my throat and I kept swallowing, trying to get it to move, and then it started foaming. A little bit of foam came out of my mouth, but most of it went up my nose and it felt like it filled my whole head. It made my eyes water like I was crying and I reached up to wipe off the water and I stuck my fingers in through the holes where my glasses should of had glass.

Francisco just stood there looking at me and he had such a goofy expression on his face that I started laughing like a maniac. I laughed and laughed because it was really pretty funny except that it kind of hurt. But it didn't hurt as much as getting your glasses broke right on your face or your *cojones* kicked up into your stomach.

I picked up my books and laughed all the way over to the bus, which was just about to leave. The bus driver said, "You all right, kid?" and I said, "Yeah, I'm fine," which was true except for having a fizzy head. Nobody sat near me on the bus to Tío's house and nobody sat near me the next day, neither, on the way to school. I took another Alka-Seltzer with me, just in case, but I never had to use it. After that first day, Francisco acted like he never even saw me before which was fine by me.

CHAPTER 19

LIVING IN T OR C

PRIMO WAS WRONG ABOUT INTELLECTUALS GETTING THEIR ASS kicked all the time. Except for Francisco, nobody even tried to mess with me and I'm surrounded by girls because mostly the smart kids are all girls. None of them are as smart as Lupe, though. She writes me a letter every day and I write her one back and then we mail them on Friday so we can read one letter every day until we get the next envelope, but I always read them all at once. And I read them all over again every day, too. Lupe writes just as good as the people who write our books in school, so I always make sure I spell everything right and use my good grammar so she'll know I'm not a *menso*. At first, I kept Lupe's letters under my pillow but pretty soon there were so many it was making my neck hurt, so I stuck them under my mattress for sweet dreams.

I don't have to stick Lupe's letters under the mattress to hide them from Tío because he doesn't even snoop in my room. He trusts me. Like he told me I couldn't use the Internet to send any e-mails, just to surf the Internet for school projects or else read the news. I figured he would check up on me, but he hardly even uses his computer. I thought about sneaking one little e-mail to Lupe but I didn't do it because Mr. G looks like the kind of father who would say he trusts you but he would still check up on you just in case and if he saw my e-mail then he would know I'm a sneaky liar and not the kind of man he can respect. Plus, I gave Tío my word of honor and I wouldn't break it even if I didn't care about Mr. G.

Every day, I have to come straight home from school and help Tío who is already home because he starts work at five o'clock in the morning. Tío doesn't sit around after work and watch TV sports or hang out in the bar like a normal bachelor. He does projects. Hard projects that make you sweat, like building a cement block wall or hauling a bunch of eight-by-eights down to the river and digging up some dirt so we can put them along the trail to make a nice border. Tío doesn't eat like a normal bachelor, neither. Instead of burritos and cheeseburgers and beers, he eats organic brown rice and vegetables and when he makes a barbecue, he fires up some salmon steaks instead of real steaks. He drinks iced tea that smells funny, a little bit like old socks, but it doesn't taste too bad and it makes you feel calm and smooth inside because it's herbalized and doesn't have caffeine which is a artificial

141

stimulant. I thought I would get even skinnier eating this kind of food, but I'm getting thicker in some places. It must be all that work Tío makes me do and no sodas or chips to be found in this whole house because I checked.

Tío won't let me watch regular TV, neither, just PBS or BBC. Not for a punishment, though. More like for principles. Tío has more principles than anybody I ever knew. He says TV rots your brain and the commercials make you think you need stuff you don't need because you wouldn't even know that stuff existed if you didn't see it on TV, so how could you need it. Plus he says there's enough violence in the world already without making up more for the TV addicts. I was pretty surprised but after only about two days, I stopped missing TV. I like it better to just walk down by the river and think. Sometimes I sit on one of the picnic tables under the trees and read a book or write a poem for Lupe or sometimes just sit and let my brain float down the river like a fat lazy duck. At first, the river was real low and sad-looking and the coyotes could walk right out in the middle and catch a fish, which I saw with my own eyes one day, but pretty soon the rains started up in the mountains and then they opened up the dam so the ranchers could irrigate and now the Rio Grande really looks like a river somebody would sing a song about.

One day I got up when Tío did just to see how it feels to be awake that early and then he left for work and I went outside because I never saw a sunrise before when I was sober.

Now I know what people are talking about when they say the light in New Mexico is different from anyplace else so all the artists like to move here. Even though I never been to another state, I could tell the light was special because the whole world turned kind of yellow with pink around the edges. Then I saw this bird that was bigger than any bird I ever saw, with a real long neck and a black ring around its eye. It flew right over my head and I could hear the wings flapping so loud it sounded like they were hydraulic. If you never saw a big bird in a real quiet place then you don't know they make all that noise when they fly around, kind of like if you see one of those programs on PBS where the ballerinas are dancing, if you turn off the sound they look light and fluffy but if you turn up the sound they sound like an elephant stomping around. That bird was a blue heron. I looked it up in one of Tío's books. He has about a thousand books, mostly about animals and places you can go camping and backpacking where you have to bring everything yourself including toilet paper and a little shovel to dig a toilet pit and you have to watch out for bears and mountain lions.

When I asked Tío wasn't he afraid to go someplace where a mountain lion might chew off his leg, he said he would take his chances against a mountain lion any day instead of a punk with a gun in his hand and a head full of hate. Tío talks like that sometimes, like a poem. Beecher would probably like him. Lots of women like him. I can tell by the way they look at him when we go to a store or something, but he doesn't have a girlfriend and he never got married. For a while I was wondering was he gay and I decided even if he was it didn't matter because he wasn't a pervert who would do something bad to me, but then one morning I woke up and I saw this real fine lady tiptoeing outside to her car and Tío standing at the window drinking his stinky herbalized tea and watching her go.

Keeping my word of honor about not sending e-mails turned out real good because yesterday Tío said I could e-mail Lupe because I been doing so good in school that my new English teacher called up my parents and told them I'm an excellent student and a good example for the other kids, which is what you would call irony if it was in your literature book. When Papi called me up and said he got a call from one of my teachers, I started to feel like I was going to throw up all that brown rice that Tío's been feeding me. But then he said, "Your mother is so proud of you, son," and I knew he meant he was, too, except he isn't too good at saying that kind of stuff. I'm not, neither. Like I never thanked him for being a good dad who cares about his kids. So I told him thanks for sending me to stay with Tío where I could get rehabilitated and not turn into a incorrigible juvenile delinquent who is a shame to the whole family.

Living with Tío is interesting even if it isn't too normal. Like on this one weekend, he took me to this bathhouse in T or C, downtown in a real old kind of crumbly place where the bath part looked like those real old showers they have at the gym, where they look dirty even if you scrub them every day, but Tío said don't worry; there's no germs because the water is 115 degrees right out of the ground. That water is supposed to have some kind of miracle minerals that heal you if you got achy bones or some kind of sickness that the doctors don't know. The whole downtown of T or C has way-hot water under it, so if you live down there, you can go out in your backyard and dig a well and have your own personal hot tub.

Inside the bathhouse, we went to the men's section where there were five bathtubs made all out of tile with real big faucets. You could close a long curtain in front of your bathtub so you could take off all your clothes and nobody could see you unless they drilled a little hole in the wall to peek through like they do in those creepy motels. There was a little hole in the wall between my bathtub and the next bathtub, so I hung my towel over the hole. It's a good thing they had a cold-water faucet on that bathtub because that water was H-O-T *caliente*. It shriveled me up and turned me red and wrinkled like a little baby, but after a couple minutes I started to like it. I laid back in the water and floated like an old stick and pretty soon I felt my brain start floating, too. I got the same feeling I get when Lupe kisses me real soft like a feather.

After ten minutes, Tío knocked on my curtain and said I had to get out of the water because it was my first time. Besides, we had to take a shower and get dressed because Tío was going to drop me off at the Black Cat so I could hear the poetry reading while he went grocery shopping and changed the oil in his truck. I would of chickened out from going to the poetry reading except when I told Tío I might go there sometime, he offered to drop me off and I didn't want to look like a little kid afraid to do something just because he never did it before.

There was a sign on the door of the bookstore that said WELCOME TO COFFEE AND CONFUSION: OPEN MIKE. At first, I was kind of nervous to go in there because there weren't any other kids, just old people and most of them pretty white. But then I saw that a bunch of the old men had ponytails and a couple people looked like they could even be Mexican. So I went and stood inside the door and I heard this one old hippie-looking dude in a black baseball cap talking to this lady with white hair who looked like a grandmother, except the dude said, "The lemmings don't give a shit because they don't know shit and then they get in your shit and talk shit about you," and the lady didn't scream or tell him to clean up his language. She just laughed. Then the owner of the bookstore with the long yellow hair saw me and waved at me and pointed to a chair in the corner. So I sat down and waited.

Pretty soon this real skinny old dude with a little white goatee got up and started reading a poem about some black dude beating him up when he was in school and after that they got to be friends. Then another old guy with purple hair got up and read a poem about doesn't it break your heart to live in a country that is a country apart from the rest of the world because of the war in Iraq, and everybody clapped a lot.

Then this lady with pink glasses and wearing a long skirt but a man's shirt got up and played her guitar and made everybody sing "I wanna go home" every couple seconds. After that, a real short lady from Iran read this poem about how home isn't where you live, it's where you love. She first read the poem in her own language and even though I couldn't understand it, I could tell it sounded better before she turned it into English. Just like when you have a song in Spanish where the words say, "I'm a sincere man from the land of the palm trees and before I die, I want to share the poetry in my soul. My poetry is clear green and burning red, my poetry is a wounded deer that you seek in the forest," when they translate it to English they say, "I write my songs with no learning and yet with truth they are burning," just to make a rhyme out of it.

After that, about fifteen more people read their poems and stories. It was sort of weird but it was nice to be sitting in a place where everybody was laughing and feeling happy about listening to each other read and nobody making fun of each other even if the stuff they wrote wasn't too good or they had a squeaking voice or made a mistake and had to read something over twice.

Right at the end, the skinny guy with the goatee got up and said, "We have a new reader this week. Her name is Ramona and she just moved here from North Carolina. Let's give her a warm welcome." Everybody clapped real polite and this lady went up to the front. She had short brown hair, not flat and shiny but sticking up all over the place like little chocolate curls. She said, "I have never read in front of an audience before, so please excuse me if I blush." You could tell she was nervous because her face looked like she just ate a habanero chile but the rest of her was the same color as a peach. She talked with a big Southern accent like I never heard except in the movies. And she read this story she wrote about how books changed her life. I even remember part of it. She said, "I just love books. I love everything about them, the way they look and smell and feel. And sometimes, when I'm fixin' to start reading a new book, I sit and hold it in my hands awhile and think about it, the way some folks sit and ponder their travel brochures. And when I open a new book, I always hope that the words will capture me and carry me off to some new place and that when I get there, I will be far, far away from me."

I knew exactly what she meant which was weird because there she was, this kind of old Anglo lady from thousands of miles away with a whole different kind of life from me, but she told a story that could have came out of my own mouth.

CHAPTER 20

THE BLACK CAT

LAST SUNDAY, THERE WAS ANOTHER POETRY READING AT THE Black Cat and Tío didn't even ask me if I wanted to go. He just said what time does it start and was I going to read any of my poems. Tío is the only person except Lupe who ever read my poems. He said he doesn't know diddly-squat about poetry but he thought they were pretty good. *Diddly-squat* is the kind of thing Tío gets from working around too many Anglos and he thinks it's real funny to copy their accent. He's always saying things like "Get 'er done" and "Well, I'll be danged."

I don't even get nervous going to the Black Cat anymore because I went there a couple of times just to look around, and one day when there wasn't anybody else in there, that lady with the yellow hair told me her name was Rhonda and she asked me did I want some coffee because it was on the house since she was going to empty out the coffeepot pretty soon. I took the coffee because I didn't want to hurt her feelings after she told me her name and everything, but I had to dump it out in the bathroom because it tasted so bad. I never drank coffee before. It smells kind of good but it's one of those things like vanilla or whisky that if you drink it straight, you'll be sorry.

I took one of my poems to the reading, but I didn't sign up my name to read. I couldn't stand there in front of all those people and read something so personal. I been thinking maybe I would write something about the river or that blue heron or something that wasn't about me so maybe I could read it. That North Carolina lady, Ramona, was there again and I sat in the chair next to her except I didn't say anything, just sat there and smelled her perfume which smelled exactly like Lupe so I felt happy and sad both at the same time. Ramona read another story about this girl who was seventeen and went to visit her brother who was in the Navy. The girl decided she was tired of being a virgin, so she spent the whole night with a sailor who thought she was beautiful. When her brother found out he said he would kill that guy and he choked his sister and then he started crying. Even though it was a pretty sad story, Ramona told it real funny and everybody laughed so loud.

The next weekend after that, Tío and me drove over to Rosablanca to visit my family. Even though it's only a couple months since I saw them, they looked different, especially my parents. They didn't used to have wrinkles or gray hairs. Letty and Juanito kept hanging on my arms and legs and asking me did I want to play a game or they showed me all the junky stuff they made in art class in school. I told them to stop because they gave me a pain in the ass but they probably knew I was just saying that stuff so I wouldn't feel like crying because they just laughed and didn't let go.

Tío let me borrow his truck and Mr. G let me drive Lupe over to Caliche's for a frozen custard. At first, I felt kind of shy but as soon as we got around the corner from her house, Lupe hollered, "Pull over. Quick!" so I hit the brakes. As soon as we pulled to the curb, Lupe jumped in my lap and kissed me all over my face and neck and ears. I told her she scared me and I thought it was a real emergency and she said, "You don't think this is an emergency?" and kissed me some more until it was a real emergency and we had to go get that custard to cool us down.

After we ate our custard, Lupe wiped her mouth real careful with a napkin and then she leaned over and put her hands on my face and I thought she was going to kiss me except she said, "Eddie, I have to tell you something and it's real bad." For a second, my brain started yelling, "Pregnant!" but that couldn't happen unless Lupe was messing around on me and I knew she wasn't, so then I started thinking maybe she got a new boyfriend while I was gone, but she said, "Primo got busted."

"Which Primo?" I said, except I knew she would say Enrique because I already heard my parents whispering about it and Mami said, "Don't tell him. He's doing so well in school." Enrique got busted for stealing car stereos and selling them which isn't like a major crime, but he already got busted twice before for some other stuff and once when he got caught shoplifting, he had a gun stuck in his sock. He was a little kid back then so he didn't do any time, but once you got a weapon on your record, the cops watch out for you to grow up and then they get you if you keep on engaging in criminal activities. I told Primo he should go to TVI like Miguel did and get a job in electronics like they show on the commercials but he said he already wasted too much of his life in school and why would anybody go to school if they didn't have to, especially if they had to pay money to go.

"Sorry, Eddie," Lupe said. And I thought she would say something like she usually says, like Primo has the same options as everybody else, but he always takes the easy way, the shortcuts, because he's in too big of a hurry to stop and think about what he's doing and he thinks he's so slick that he'll never get busted even after he just got busted. But Lupe didn't say anything. She didn't start crying or try to cheer me up or try to pretend like it was no big deal. She just sat there and let things be quiet, which is one of the best things about her. She knows when to shut up and she can shut up for a real long time, too, and not get mad about it after.

When I dropped Lupe off at her house, she kissed me on

the nose and said, "Ay *te watcho*" and jumped out of the truck. She always tells me, "Ay *te watcho*," which means "Watch yourself," instead of saying something romantic like "I'll miss you" or "I can't wait until I see you again."

I hollered out the window that most girls would probably cry if their boyfriend got sent way over the mountains where she couldn't see him. Lupe came around to the driver's side and stuck her head inside the window and said even if she couldn't see me, she could hear my heart beating at night when she put her head on her pillow. "Besides," she said, "how could I be sad when every time I see you, you're like a new version of my old boyfriend except you get better every time?" Then she walked into her house and didn't even turn around, just swished her *nalgas* back and forth to say *hasta luego*.

When I was over in Rosablanca, I took my journal to the library, too. I walked right in the front door and up to the desk and said could I please speak to Miss Beecher and when she came out, I handed my journal to her just like I planned in my intention. I didn't have to remind her my name, though, because as soon as Beecher saw me, she said, "Hello, Eddie." She started to open my journal but I asked her would she please read it later when I wasn't standing there feeling so nervous. She closed it right away and sort of wrapped her arms around it like a hug. Then I told her how she was the best teacher and I was thinking on going to college but I would need a good recommendation, so could she please consider writing one for me. Then I started thinking maybe she would think I said she was the best teacher I ever had just so she would write me a recommendation.

"Even if you don't want to recommend me, I still meant what I said about you being the best teacher," I told her.

"I know you aren't a manipulative person, Eddie," Beecher said. "And I would be delighted to write you a recommendation. I hope you go to college and earn your PhD in English so you can be a literature professor someday. Unless you'd rather be a high school teacher because you like high school so much." Then she laughed out loud for a minute until she remembered we were at the library, so she put her hand over her mouth and kept on laughing so her hair shook all around her face with little shivers like it was laughing, too.

I know Beecher was just joking about me being a teacher, but all the way driving back to T or C, I kept remembering what she said and having a little picture in my mind of me being a teacher. I would let people write whatever they wanted to, just like Beecher did, and if they said they didn't care if they graduated, I would make them read *The Four Agreements* so they could learn how to think impeccable thoughts. I don't think I would ever be a teacher, but a lot of things have happened lately that I never would of believed if you told me they were going to happen, so I'm not making any promises to myself. Except I did make one kind of promise, though. I decided that I'm never going to jail unless it's one of those situations where the cops bust you just for being the wrong color in the wrong place at the wrong time.

I had so many things to think about after that visit and I had a lot of time to think on the way back because Tío likes to listen to music while he's driving, so he doesn't care if you don't talk to him. He was listening to this cassette he bought off a guy who works at Mail Boxes Etc. who is in this band called Caliente! The music was pretty good so we didn't say anything all the way across 70 East from Alamogordo past White Sands and almost to Cruces. Right when we started to go through that pass where the Organ Mountains start to look real sharp and pretty, Tío turned down the music and said, "You know, Eddie, it's okay if you're still a virgin."

At first, I thought I was tripping because why would Tío say something like that when we never even said one word about sex in the whole time I been at his house. He could have figured it out from reading me and Lupe's letters, but I knew he didn't read them. I was going to say, "What makes you think I'm a virgin?" but I didn't want to hear the answer so I didn't say anything. Then Tío said, "Sorry if I stepped on your toes there, bud. Just wanted you to know you aren't the Lone Ranger even if you think you are. Most of the guys your age who brag about all the pussy they're getting aren't getting any or they would keep their mouths shut so other guys won't go after their women."

I still didn't know what to say. Me and Lupe got real close a couple times, but we never had official sex because she's

Catholic so she couldn't have an abortion and if she had a baby and we got married then she would end up hating me after she got tired of getting up in the middle of the night to feed a baby who was crying when she should have been in college learning how to be the doctor who delivers the babies.

Tío probably figured he was right since I didn't say anything because he said, "Take your time, *mijo*. Take your time." He played a little drums on the steering wheel, then he turned down the music even lower. "I know you think you and Lupe will love each other for the rest of your life and maybe you will. But your hormones are in control right now, so you could start confusing lust and love. Not that you can't have both, but at your age, lust takes priority." He sounded just like Beecher when he said that. I started thinking maybe I should introduce them because Beecher is the only lady I know who is as smart as Tío and she eats the same kind of weird healthy food like he does and I bet she doesn't watch TV, neither.

"Don't worry," I told Tío. "Me and Lupe aren't taking any chances, if that's what you're worried about."

"Lupe reminds me of your mother, you know," Tío said, which made me wonder if maybe he drank some beers out back with Papi before we left. "Your mother was the smartest girl in the whole school. Did you know that? Sharp as a razor blade. When she started dating your father, I was so jealous. I wished I had found her first. She was so hot she sizzled." Tío licked his finger and stuck it on his leg and made a fat-in-the-fire sound. "She could have gone to college. She could have been the first woman president. She could have done anything, but she married your dad and then you came along and then Letty and Juanito." I didn't say anything because I was still trying to picture my mother as a hot babe genius instead of a old lady in a hairnet dishing up macaronis and *queso* for little kids in the school cafeteria or roasting chiles in the kitchen at home, but Tío probably thought he hurt my feelings because he quick looked over at me and said, "Hey. She loves you. I'm not saying she's not happy. But I always wonder if she might have been even happier if she had the chance to fly as high as her wings could have taken her."

And I started thinking of all the times I would come into the house and my mother would be standing in the living room staring at the television except it wasn't turned on, or else she would be standing in the middle of the kitchen not even cooking and if I asked her what was she thinking, she would jump a little bit like I scared her and I would have to ask her again and she would say, "Oh, nothing." And I wondered if maybe she had been thinking that her life was nothing, except her life isn't nothing because if it wasn't for her, I would have been a pretty bad criminal or at least dropped out of school and my father would have probably had to go to jail for losing his temper and punching the wrong guy. But maybe saving a couple of loser men and cooking the best chile rellenos in the neighborhood doesn't feel like something so big to a woman with a brain as sharp as a razor blade.

That's when I decided not to ask Lupe to marry me until I'm twenty-one and a big success, or at least a medium-size one. I made the intention to keep on loving Lupe but not hold her back even one little bit. I'll try to go to college with her but if she gets a scholarship to some big fancy school, I will tell her go ahead and be a doctor and open her wings and fly. And I'll go to NMSU and I'll keep writing her one letter a day and I'll write her a bunch of poems, too, enough to make a whole book. And I'll get a good job and make a real nice house so after Lupe is done flying, she'll have a place to make a nest if she wants to. Who knows—I might even do a little bit of flying myself.

CHAPTER 21

MAN-TO-MAN

EVERY ONCE IN A WHILE, PAPI TRIES TO HAVE A MAN-TO-MAN with me, but he doesn't try too hard because it's usually Mami's idea and we both know it. Plus, he had a way different life from me so he doesn't usually get it why I do what I do. Like for example him and his brothers grew up on a ranch over by Portales which is practically Texas, so they all dress like old-time *caballeros* with jeans real long that bunch up around their ankles so when they sit in the saddle, they won't look like *mensos* wearing high-waters. And they wear those thick cotton shirts that you have to iron after you wash them, and they're too hot for the desert but they keep out the bugs and if they ride past a mesquite bush too close, their arms don't get all scratched up.

Papi's always telling me to tuck in my shirt, but for one thing, my shirts are too long to tuck in and if I did tuck them in, I'd look like a *gordo* even though I'm skinny because my pants would be all full of shirt. Or I would have to buy those different shirts like Harvey Castro wears that are real short like a girl shirt so you can tuck them in and wear a necktie and try to look like you sell insurance. If I went around looking like that, I'd get my ass kicked so fast because I'm not Harvey Castro and he isn't me. If Harvey Castro wore a big shirt, he'd look like Halloween or something, and he would lose his cool just like that. But I can't explain all that to Papi because he's too tired to sit down and listen to a real long answer. So when he asks me why don't I get a better attitude or at least tuck in my shirt, I just shrug my shoulders and look at my shoes for a minute until he says never mind what's the point in talking to somebody who never listens.

When I was over visiting Rosablanca, I could tell that Papi was trying to make the connection with me and he even acted like it was his own idea. The night before I had to go back to T or C to take my exams, Papi knocked on the door to my room which was the first time he ever knocked. He usually just barges into whatever room he wants because it's his house and he built it with his own two hands with money he busted his ass to earn so if he wants to walk into a room, he'll walk into it and you better shut up.

When Papi knocked, I was so surprised I didn't say anything for a couple seconds, just looked at him. Usually I don't look at him real close because I already know what he looks like. But this time, I looked at him like he was some guy on the street and he looked a little bit nervous which made me feel a little bit nervous, too.

"Come on in," I said, but then he did come in and there we were, standing too close to each other and no place to sit because my room is so small. I went over and shoved all the clothes off the little wood chair in the corner and Papi sat down on it which made him look even more nervous than he did when he was standing up. I went over and sat down on the bed and tried to look Papi in the eye but if you look a man like Papi in the eye for too long, he usually thinks you want to hit him, so I stopped looking at him and pretended to look out the window.

Papi coughed a couple times and then he tried to have a man-to-man about the bees and the birds, but he was about ten years too late. When I told Papi that he didn't have to fill me in on women and sex and all that stuff, because Primo already told me everything I need to know, Papi looked kind of worried for a minute, but then he smiled.

"Well, Enrique probably knows more what he's talking about than I do when it comes to women," Papi said.

We both laughed like he was right, but after Papi left I started thinking he was wrong. Mami loves him so much that sometimes she gets up right in the middle of eating dinner and goes over and kisses him on top of his head. My mother is one of those women who you are lucky if you even get to know them. But if you are a man who gets to marry them and they're still *enamorada* with you after almost twenty years, then you must know something about women.

Primo probably didn't tell me exactly the same stuff that Papi would have, but he filled in all the blanks. After he explained the different body parts and what they do, he filled me in on female psychology, too. Like one thing girls hate so much is if you ask them for their phone number and then don't call them. They get all mad because they think you just wanted to see if you could get their number. They don't know that the reason you don't call them is maybe you don't got a cool car to pick them up in or any money to take them out someplace nice or you aren't too good at making conversation with girls who are so pretty that you can't concentrate when you look at them.

"It's better if you give them your cell phone number," Primo says. "That way, they can call you up and flirt with you and stuff, but you never ask them out so they think you're too cool for them or else you got a jealous girlfriend who will slit their throat or something. And if they ask you out, you don't say anything for a long time and they start thinking that maybe they aren't as hot as they thought they were. Then pretty soon they stop calling you. Or you just stop taking their calls and they get mad at you and tell all the other girls what a macho jerk you are which makes the other girls want you even more."

When I first got Lupe for a girlfriend, Primo kept telling

me to keep my options open and not get chained to one girl, even if she was hot, because she would make that chain a little bit shorter every day until the next thing you know, you can't even take a piss without permission.

"I'm not on any chain," I told Primo, and he said, "You keep on thinking that, dude. Enjoy your illusions."

I don't think I'm illusioning anything. Lupe and me respect each other and if I need to go do something by myself, I do it and she doesn't say anything. She's too busy doing homework and learning to play the piano and doing yoga exercises so she can stay in touch with her peaceful center to worry about what I'm doing every single second. Primo said that proves she doesn't really care about me. He said if a girl really loves you, she'll get jealous and pitch a fit if you don't act like you're thinking about her all the time, even when you're sleeping. She'll make you check in every twenty-four hours like she's your parole officer. And if she catches you checking out the *chichis* on some other girl, she won't let you touch hers for two days just to punish you.

"But Lupe isn't the jealous type," I told Primo.

"All women are the jealous type," he said. "It's in their hormones. If Lupe isn't jealous, then she probably has another boyfriend. Or maybe she secretly likes girls."

I told Primo he was full of shit, but for a little while after that, I started watching Lupe and checking out how she acted if I looked at another girl. And I watched to see did her face change when she looked at some real popular guy who has a hot car and a wallet full of twenties. I even smiled at Silvia Miranda one day right in front of Lupe to see what she would do.

Lupe and I were eating lunch on the playground behind the tennis courts at school and Silvia came out and sat down on one of the weird old swings and started kicking her feet to try to make it go. Silvia looked over at us and I smiled at her and I checked out Lupe in the corner of my eye. She just took another bite of her chocolate chip cookie like it was nothing. She even waved at Silvia. One of those little finger wiggles like girls do when they see one of their friends.

"You know her?" I asked Lupe.

"Not really," Lupe said, "but she looks nice. Do you know her?"

"Yeah, I guess. I been going to school with her since we were little kids."

Lupe didn't say anything else and she didn't ask any questions about Silvia even though I thought she would because Silvia is real pretty. Not beautiful like Lupe, but pretty enough that she could be a model or a movie star if she doesn't turn out to be a *gordita* like her mother. All the Miranda girls start out looking real good but something happens to them when they turn eighteen. They puff up like *sopapillas*.

"I guess you aren't the jealous type, huh?" I said to Lupe. She quick looked at Silvia and back at me.

"Should I be jealous?"

"No," I said.

"You sure?"

"No. For reals."

"Then why did you just ask me if I'm the jealous type?" When Lupe gets a question in her head, she doesn't let it go until she figures it out and she can always tell if you're just making up an answer, even if you make up a real good one that your parents would believe. She probably gets that from watching her father the killer lawyer.

"I just wondered. That's all." I looked Lupe straight in the eye so she could see I was telling the truth. She studied me like a book for a couple seconds and then she said, "Do you want to know why I'm not jealous, Eddie?"

I wasn't sure I wanted to know the answer but I knew if I said never mind, I'd be in big trouble because I'm the one who brought up the whole subject.

"I'm not jealous because I'm really smart and I'm not bad-looking and I really really really care about you," Lupe said. "I'm a wonderful girlfriend to you. And if you didn't appreciate me enough to be faithful, then you would be too stupid to have for a boyfriend."

When I told Primo what Lupe said, he was smoking a cigarette and he cracked up so hard I swear I saw smoke coming out of his ears.

"Man!" he said in between choking. He slapped me on the back real hard. "You got your hands full, Primito." He choked some more and then he said, "Does she got any sisters?"

I wish Lupe did have a sister because that would be so cool if she had a sister who liked Primo, except I don't think a sister of Lupe's would like Primo because he's too slick, or at least he thinks he is. If he really was slick he wouldn't be sitting in jail right now, waiting to find out whether he's going to get three years or life on account of he's on his third strike.

CHAPTER 22

SUNGLASSES FOR BOOKS

I DON'T LIKE TO GO TO A JAIL EVEN IF I'M ON THE RIGHT SIDE of the bars because I always think the cops could just come up and throw me inside and how would I ever get out. But I couldn't leave Primo sitting there thinking everybody finally gave up on caring about him, like his parents who washed him off their hands.

In the movies they always have a little phone booth with a window to talk through, but the Rosablanca jail just has a big room with some cheap tables and plastic chairs where the visitors can talk to the prisoners while some real big guys with guns stand around and pretend they aren't listening to every word. Primo didn't have much to say, though, after he said, "Wassup?" He looked at me for about half a second and then he looked in some other direction to give me a chance to check him out and get over it. He didn't want to see me looking at him.

I never visited Primo before when he got busted because my parents wouldn't let me, so I never saw him without his cool clothes and his hair all combed just right and his designer shades. Even those dumb jail clothes couldn't make him look ugly, though, because he's the kind of guy who looks good no matter what. From across the room, he looked pretty much the same. But when he started shuffling over to the table where I was sitting, with handcuffs on his hands and feet, I felt kind of sick to my stomach because I could see he lost his attitude. Primo always wears his attitude like a coat he picks up and puts on whenever he goes out the door.

I leaned down and scratched my ankle for a second so I could get my face straight and after that I kept it straight the whole time, no matter what I was feeling inside.

After he finally sat down I said, "Hey, 'Rique, I sent you a book, but they sent it back." And he said, "Yeah, you got to send books straight from the publisher. They're afraid you'll dust the pages with cocaine or heroin or something."

"What kind of stupid idiot would mail drugs to a jail?" I said and he said, "You'd be surprised," which I probably would because I bet a lot of people are that stupid or at least a couple people were or the cops wouldn't have made up that rule.

I told Primo I didn't know how to get a book from a publisher but I would see if I could find out and he said, "Don't waste your time." I told him it wouldn't be a waste of time because the one I sent was a real good book, one of the best books I ever read, and it was real short but it could change your life. The whole time I was talking, Primo sat there shaking his head, back and forth, real slow, looking down at the table or up at the ceiling.

"What?" I said. "It's a good book. I'm telling you."

"I bet it is," he said. He kind of smiled at the wall, but not happy. Then all of a sudden he looked me right in the eye and pinned me to my chair. "I never read a book in my life."

I didn't say anything for a minute because what can you say to a person who just told you they never read a book in their whole life and you can tell they aren't joking or lying or trying to look cool? After a couple seconds, I started to ask him why didn't he like to read, and then I stopped because I don't know how I knew it, but I knew it. Primo never read a book because he can't read.

"Big tragedy, huh?" he said, with that same weird smile, so I knew he knew what I was thinking. He usually does. He might not be able to read a book but he can read my mind so fast, almost as fast as I can read it myself.

"Yeah," I said, because it really is a tragedy in my mind. I tried to think about what my life would be like if I didn't read so many books, like what I would do if I couldn't open a book and just disappear inside it when I needed to.

"Hey, lighten up," Primo said. "I was kidding. It's no big deal. Books are boring, compared to real life."

I was going to argue with him, but then I decided not to because even if I said the names of some real good books, he wouldn't believe they were good. And even if I won the argument, what would I win? Nothing. Just like it said in that article that McElroy made us read.

"Hey, don't let me be a bad influence on you," Primo said. "I know you like school, dude, and that's okay. You just keep on studying and go to college or whatever because if you get stupid and decide to get married, you're going to need a good job. If your little girlfriend really does get to be a doctor someday, you can't be going around mowing people's lawns."

I don't just mow lawns. I started to tell him about all the other things I do, like plant seedlings and build rock walls to prevent soil erosion and prune trees to their best shape, but Primo held up his handcuffs.

"Dude, it doesn't matter how much work you do. It matters how much paper you got. If you don't got a college degree, then you mow lawns for a living. If you go to college, then you're a landscape architect. No difference in the work. Big difference in the paycheck."

"Yeah," I said, "well if you're so smart, why don't you go to college?"

"I never said I wasn't smart," Primo said. "Shit, I'm probably some kind of genius."

He probably is a genius, just like Harvey Castro. Every time *mi tía* Carolina comes over to drink coffee with my mother, she asks how are me and Letty and Juanito doing in school so she can brag about how Enrique was so much smarter than the other kids that they skipped him out of first grade right up to third grade.

"So, at least get your GED while you're in here, Mr. Genius," I told Primo. "Don't they got those programs?"

Primo sat back hard in his chair. "Teachers are a pain in the ass. Besides, reading gives me a headache. So, let's change the subject, okay?"

We changed the subject and talked about *nuestra familia* and what was going on, but my brain kept thinking about what Primo said, that reading gives him a headache. And that reminded me of when Beecher first came to our class and Jaime kept sneaking his sunglasses on whenever Beecher wasn't looking. Most of the teachers would confiscate your shades or send you to the office, but Beecher just walked over to Jaime and took his sunglasses right off his face and handed him a blue plastic page that you could see through.

"Try this," she said, and Jaime just looked at her, so she opened his book and put the plastic over the page. "Just try it, okay?"

Jaime always used to say he was allergic to reading. I must have tried to get him to read a hundred books since the time we knew each other, but he never read a single one. When Beecher put that blue plastic on his book, Jaime looked over at me but I didn't help him out because I was on Beecher's side that time. I wanted him to try it, too. So, finally he did. He read for a couple minutes and then he looked at Beecher again but not like she was crazy, more like she was a magician or something.

Beecher left that blue sheet on Jaime's page and told us about how there's a lot of kids who everybody thinks they're dumb but they really have some kind of problem with the lights in school because they aren't the right color. Like if girls put on makeup it looks good at home but when they get to school, their face looks yellow or blue because of those lights. And Beecher said some kids always want to wear sunglasses or hats pulled way down over their eyes and they hate reading and sometimes they end up in special ed or juvi because they act so bad whenever they have to read. Beecher handed out some clear plastic pages in all kinds of colors—red and purple and blue and gray—to all the kids who hate reading, so they wouldn't get a headache.

"They won't let you wear sunglasses in school," Beecher said, "but there's no rule that says your book can't wear sunglasses."

Probably half the kids in that class started using those plastics and a lot of them stopped hating to read, and Teeny White asked Beecher why didn't the school just change the lights if they gave so many kids a headache. Beecher said our school system is a bureaucracy and it isn't that easy to change things in a bureaucracy, plus some people didn't believe the plastics could work so easy because they weren't scientific enough.

Too bad Primo didn't get to be in Beecher's class, because

she probably could have made him like reading, just like Jaime. I didn't tell Primo about the lights and the plastic pages because I knew he wouldn't believe me. It sounds like some kind of fishy story that you have to see it to believe it. But the jail has the same kind of lights as school, so I decided to show Primo instead of tell him. I decided to get one of those pages and send it to him so he could try it out with nobody watching him so he wouldn't have to act all cool, but the jail would probably send the page back if I mailed it, and besides, I wasn't sure where to find one.

So I decided I'm going to ask Beecher to get one of those plastics for Primo because the cops would probably let her give it to him because she's a librarian who used to be a real teacher. And if they won't, she's smart enough to figure out how to get one for him. And I'm going to ask her how to get a publisher to send a book to somebody in jail, too. I have some money saved up, so I can send him a lot of different books, but nothing too easy because then he'd just get pissed off. I think the first book should be *The Curious Incident of the Dog in the Night-Time* because the kid in that book is really smart except everybody thinks he's stupid so Primo could probably relate.

Primo might not open the packages. And even if he does, he might not read the books. But he's smart, so I know if he makes the intention to learn how to read, he can do it. I wish I could make the intention for him, but it doesn't work that way. And if I bug him about it, he won't do it just to be stubborn because he hates when anybody tries to tell him what to do.

That's probably the worst thing about being in jail. He'll probably get used to crappy food and a hard bed and having to live with a bunch of weird people and some of them might try to kiss him but he's smart enough to figure how to play that one out. But I don't think Primo could ever get used to having somebody else tell him what to do and how to do it and when to do it all day long every single day. He's going to have to figure some way to keep from going crazy. And I'll keep on visiting him and writing him letters and sending him books, except when I visit him I won't ask him about the letters or the books. I'll just sit there and let him read my mind.

CHAPTER 23

LUPE'S HEART

IF NEW MEXICO DIDN'T HAVE SUCH LAME LAWS ABOUT DRUNK driving, the guy who already had six DUIs would have been in jail instead of on the road where he crashed into Lupe's mom and killed her and broke Lupe's heart. And if Lupe and her dad didn't move to Rosablanca to try to make a happier life, and if Crazy Cheyenne didn't beat up Lupe so many times, Lupe wouldn't have transferred to Bright Horizons. And if that mean teacher didn't twist my ear and make me so mad that I started hating school, I probably would have been hanging with Harvey Castro at the regular high school and trying to be a valedictorian instead of a juvenile delinquent, so I wouldn't have gone to Bright Horizons, neither. And if Beecher didn't tell us guys that we would probably get girlfriends if we signed up for ballroom dance, and if Mami didn't tell me how romantic it was when Papi used to take her dancing, then I wouldn't have signed up for dance class. And if I didn't, then I probably would never have met Lupe or if I did meet her, I would have been doing something like pounding somebody into the ground or getting dragged out of English class by the cops for shoplifting or some other thing that wouldn't have impressed her so much like I impressed her by being able to waltz.

But maybe if all those things didn't happen, I still would have met Lupe anyways if I decided to like myself enough so I could make the intention to find a wonderful girlfriend. I've been reading a lot of books about energy and the law of attraction and karma and all that woo-woo stuff. Some of it makes sense but some of it makes me laugh so hard, like I'm reading a comic book.

I thought if I read enough books, I would figure everything out, but the more I read, looking for answers, the more questions I have. I wish there was somebody who had all the answers to the questions—somebody I don't know, because if you've been talking about normal stuff with your parents all your life, like can you borrow the car and why can't you stay out past eleven on school nights and why do you have to eat broccoli, you can't walk up to your mother one day and say, "Do you think that all the energy in the universe is connected?" because she'll think you've been smoking weed or something. And if you asked your father does he think you keep getting sent back to Earth in a human form so you can learn enough lessons so your soul can go flying around enjoying itself instead of worrying about all these problems, I don't know what he would do, but it probably wouldn't be good and I'm not going to ask Papi and find out.

Sometimes me and Lupe talk about that stuff, but she has more questions than I do and she's so smart that her questions are real hard, like if something kills one person but saves a thousand people, is it all right to kill that one person.

I wish I could kill the guy who crashed into Lupe's mother. I would kill him in a heartbeat. But I never told Lupe that because she already forgave the guy and she said it made her feel a lot better and I don't want to make her feel bad again. She said she used to cry every single night for four years after her mother died because she didn't get to kiss her goodbye, but now she feels better because she had this dream that sounds a little bit creepy in a good way.

She told me about the dream one day at her house when we were practicing for dance class. We danced for about an hour which was actually pretty fun when there was no teacher to count one and two three or tell you to put your arm here or your foot there. When you get the hang of dancing, it's almost as good as making out which is what we usually do after we finish practicing.

"I have to tell you something," Lupe said, right after this one really long kiss that almost made me lose my mind. At first, I thought, Oh no, here it comes. I didn't have any special "it" in mind, but whenever a girl says "I have to tell you some-thing" in that certain voice, it's usually something you wish they didn't have to tell you.

"It's kind of weird," Lupe said, "so maybe I shouldn't tell you. I don't want you to think I'm crazy."

"I already think you're crazy," I said, just kidding, but Lupe pinched me on the stomach anyway. I grabbed her hands and she switched them real fast and spun around and wrapped my hands around her waist so I was standing behind her, my front to her back, and we were both hugging her.

"We have ways of making you talk," I whispered into her ear.

"Okay. Last night I dreamed I was at the airport," Lupe said, "and I was waiting to get on a plane. When they called our group to board, I couldn't find my boarding pass. I started to cry, but the ticket counter lady told me not to worry. She said she would print me up a new boarding pass after she checked everybody in. All the other passengers went down the ramp except this one lady who turned around and smiled at me. She was much taller than the other passengers, about seven feet tall, and very beautiful. She was wearing a silver cape and when she turned around, the cape swirled open and I could see that she was dressed all in silver, a long dress with sequins on the bodice so she sparkled."

Lupe twisted around so she could see my face and said, "Is this too weird?" and I said no. She let go of my hands and sat down on the couch and pulled me down beside her and tucked her feet under my legs which is her favorite way to sit when her dad isn't home. My favorite way for us to sit is laying down, but Lupe's the one who gets to pick the sitting formations because she's the one with the good self-control.

Lupe settled herself real comfortable and then she said, "Okay, so I was crying and the tall lady said, 'Did you lose something, honey?' and I said, 'Yes, I lost my boarding pass,' and I started to cry harder. She put her hand under my chin and lifted it up and kissed my face. She kissed my tears and when she kissed them, each tear turned into a tiny white butterfly. And the lady said, 'You can have my boarding pass, *mija.*'"

Lupe stopped talking for a second and her eyes filled up with tears. Then she said, "After she kissed my face, she opened her arms and wrapped her cape around us both and hugged me. It was the most wonderful hug, so filled with love, and it was so warm and so real and in the middle of the hug, I realized she was my mother and I said, 'Oh, Mama, I miss you so much,' and she said, 'I miss you, too, *mija.*'"

Lupe had to stop and get a tissue to blow her nose. I needed a tissue, too.

"Don't be sad, Eddie," Lupe said. "When I woke up, I could still feel that hug. It was so real. And I knew it was my mother and she's watching out for me. So now I won't be sad when I think of her."

I know it's good that Lupe won't be sad anymore. And I know you can't change the past and you have to learn your lessons and then let go and stop worrying or it can make you crazy. But I still wish I could fix it so that guy didn't kill Lupe's mother—even if it meant that Lupe would never move to Rosablanca to be my girlfriend. It would probably kill me, but I would give up Lupe if it would mean that she would have her mother and not a broken heart.

CHAPTER 24

TO WHOM IT MAY CONCERN

BEECHER SENT MY COPY OF HER LETTER OF RECOMMENDATION to our house in Rosablanca because when I talked to her, I didn't tell her I was staying with Tío on account of getting in so much trouble. I was just over there for a visit when I asked her, so she probably thought I was still at home where I should have been.

Anyway, my mother opened the letter because it was addressed to Eduardo Corazon which is my father's name, too. He's the senior and I'm the junior which used to be my nickname except I didn't like being called Junior because it sounds like a baby, so I would never answer when anybody called me that. Then they started calling me Eddie and I've been Eddie all these years until lately when I told the teachers and kids here in Truth or Consequences that my name is Eduardo.

For a long time, I didn't want the same name as Papi, and then for another long time, he probably didn't want me to have the same name as him, neither. Now I wouldn't mind having the same name, but who knows what he's thinking.

I don't know if Papi would want to share his name with me now, but he might, because Mami said he took a copy of Beecher's letter and folded it up and stuck it in his wallet. Beecher sent the letter and a note that said she made me ten copies so I would have enough to use for jobs and college applications. All those copies made me wonder does she think it's going to take me ten tries to find someplace that wants me or was she just being nice. I decided she was just being nice because if she thought I was a nine-time loser, she wouldn't have written me a letter in the first place.

Mami read me the whole letter over the phone. She had to start over twice because she started crying the first two times and her voice got all froggy. The letter started out by saying "To Whom It May Concern" which didn't sound too good to me, but Mami said that means the letter is for everybody in the world who wants to know what kind of character I have. Then Beecher wrote that she would recommend me as a student or an employee because I'm real smart and I'm not afraid to work hard.

That's not how she said it, though. She said, "I wholeheartedly recommend Eduardo Corazon for any course of study or profession he chooses. He is one of those students who make the sometimes difficult task of teaching high school worthwhile—he has an inquisitive mind, a quick intelligence, natural analytical ability, and a wry sense of humor. He is creative, persistent, and ethical. His self-confidence and leadership abilities will serve him well in any endeavor. Should you require further reference as to his character, please feel free to contact me at the address or phone number below."

I memorized the whole thing after Mami sent me a copy of the letter to show to Tío. And after Tío read the letter, I sent it to Lupe. I didn't ask her to show it to her father, but I knew she would. And then maybe he would stop looking at me like that the next time I see him. Maybe now he would shake my hand and say, "Con mucho gusto," like he means it instead of like he would have much gusto if I would get lost and forget about his beautiful, brilliant daughter.

After Tío read Beecher's letter, he said, "Uh-oh. Now the pressure's on, eh, bud?" and then real quick he said, "Just kidding." But I don't think Tío was kidding because it really is some kind of pressure to live up to a letter of recommendation. Kind of like you have a new reputation to maintain.

It's actually a lot easier to maintain a reputation as a intellectual than it is to keep on being a badass. When you're a badass, you have to fight a lot of guys or at least act like you will if they don't quit dogging you, and you have to watch your back 24-7 because you can't leave yourself open for even a couple seconds because that's long enough for somebody to take you down. You can never relax or let your guard down and if you ever cry, it's over.

You can maintain a reputation as a intellectual pretty easy because there's only a few kind of guys who will always try to cause you some trouble. Mostly they pick on you a couple times to see will you fight and if you won't, then they go fight with the badass guys to show how tough they are. So you don't have to fight as much as you would think once you start getting good grades and go down in the books as a brainiac. Most of the time, you don't have to do anything, just walk around and be yourself, not showing that you're smart or anything. Like if you have a really killer knife in your pocket, you don't have to go around flashing it all the time. You just relax because you know it's there if you have a real emergency and you need to whip it out and show it to somebody to make them back off.

But there is a certain kind of pressure after somebody writes a letter of recommendation about you. It's one thing for somebody to go around and say good things about you. That happens all the time and people forget real quick because who cares anyway. It's a whole nother thing for somebody to write that good stuff in a letter and address it To Whom It May Concern and sign their name so that letter will stand forever like a good kind of rap sheet. Even if you never saw that person again, their recommendation would still be out there someplace, waiting for anybody in the whole world to read about you in case they forgot all the good stuff the person said.

If somebody does that for you, then you have to walk

straight and be careful what you do because you don't want to mess it up even though the person probably wouldn't ask for their letter back and burn it if you did mess up. And they probably wouldn't write a different letter To Whom It May Concern to say they changed their mind and you're a freakin' loser and not somebody they can recommend with their whole heart.

If you did mess up, they would probably feel real bad for a while, and then they would shake their head and say, "I thought that kid had what it takes, but I guess I was wrong." And they might forget about you after a while. But you would never forget about them. And you would never forget that letter. After you memorize a letter like that, even if it doesn't stick to your brain forever, it will stick to your heart.

CHAPTER 25

C.A.N.T.

TODAY I'M FEELING PRETTY LUCKY TO BE ME WHICH ISN'T WHAT I ever used to feel, but after last night I changed my mind. Tío dropped me off at the Black Cat and I bought some books to give to Lupe—*The Four Agreements* and *The Secret* and *Ten Little Indians*—but there was a bunch of old people in there arguing about politics and a lady in the corner with a red tablecloth wrapped around her head who had a big deck of cards with pictures on them. She kept shuffling and shuffling those cards and then somebody would go over and sit down and she would tell them pick seven cards. The person would look real serious like if they picked the wrong cards their life would be over. Then the lady would nod her head and make her big earrings jingle and she'd say a bunch of horoscope stuff to them, like "Your moon is in Venus and your star is in heaven and you're going to meet somebody real nice and get rich," and they fell for it.

So I took my books outside and went over to sit on the bench beside the river to wait for Tío. I already read all those books, but they're the kind of book you can read a lot of times and you don't get tired of them. When I'm reading, my brain goes right into the book so I don't hear stuff going on around me, so I didn't hear T.J. coming. All of a sudden, this big boot stomped down on the bench beside me and knocked me right out of my book.

"Hey, asshole, what's up?" T.J. said, but I didn't answer him because sometimes if you ignore him he will just go away like a dog that finally figures out you aren't going to give it a bite of your burrito. But T.J. didn't leave. He shoved my books with his foot and knocked them on the ground.

"Oh, gee, I'm sorry," he said and I said, "What are you doing in T or C?" and he said, "Business."

"You want to make some money?" he asked me. "Some real money?" and I said, "No thanks." T.J. spit a wet one on the ground and said, "The cops might be interested in knowing that you made a certain delivery a few months ago."

"Go ahead and call them," I said. I didn't think he would call them, but I figured if he did I would call Sgt. Cabrera and tell her what happened and maybe her and Tío could figure out something. Or else I would tell my T or C cousins and they would tell our other cousins from Albuquerque, who would beat the shit out of T.J. or maybe kill him.

"You ain't fooling anybody, Corazon," T.J. said. I told him I wasn't trying to fool anybody and he said oh yes, I was, trying to act all intellectual and upright and responsible. He kicked *The Secret* real hard and it flew into a mesquite bush.

"You want to know a secret?" T.J. said. "I'll tell you a secret. Your girlfriend is screwing around on you over in Rosablanca."

For about half a second, I wondered if it was true, because that was the first week I didn't get an envelope of letters from Lupe. But then I decided to be impeccable and not think negative thoughts about Lupe because I knew it would turn out to be some guy from the post office who got tired of eating dust all day long and ditched all the mail in a Dumpster, so I didn't say anything. I just looked at T.J. and I was thinking what a loser he was—that's when he kicked me in the head and knocked me off the bench. I sat up on the ground, but I didn't stand up and fight him because I already fought T.J. so many times and he always wins. He's a lot bigger than me, plus he fights real dirty, too, like he would rather die than lose a fight even if the fight is over some stupid little thing like not letting him copy your math homework.

"You think you're all better than everybody because you got a rich girlfriend and you got a couple A's on your stupid report card!" T.J. yelled. I didn't say anything, but he kicked me in the leg pretty hard, so I had to get up. While I was trying to stand up, T.J. pulled a blade out of his pocket. I thought at first that he was just trying to look tough, like guys who flip the top of their cigarette lighters open and shut a bunch of times while they're talking to you. But he shoved me back onto the bench and stuck that knife right up to my neck and put his foot back up on the bench beside me.

I looked T.J. in the eye to show him that I wasn't afraid of him even though I was more afraid than I've ever been in my whole life up to now. I figured the best thing would be to keep T.J. talking and maybe somebody would come along and see us and maybe they would be the Good Samaritan type who wouldn't just pretend they didn't see me getting murdered.

"You're just as smart as I am," I said. "Maybe even smarter. You could get all A's if you want to. You could probably get a scholarship for college."

T.J. snorted and some little drops of water hit my face, but I didn't move.

"You could if you tried," I said. "You could get a regular job and stop dealing."

"I can't, asshole," T.J. said.

"Yes you can," I said. "You just have to make up your mind and do it."

"You don't get it, do you?" T.J. said. He leaned down real close so I could see the little red veins in his eyeballs. "I. Can't. C. A. N. T." He stuck that knife into my neck and it felt like I might be bleeding. I was thinking I would have to

189

try to take him, but then I noticed the knife was shaking a little bit and I thought for sure he was going to slice me then, and I think he would have except he started crying just a little bit and when I saw him crying I felt so sorry for him that I started crying a little bit, too. I always thought he liked being a big-shot badass criminal, but I never thought he might have gotten ambushed by those drug guys who tried to ambush me except I had cousins to back me up and T.J. is a loner for real. If you're a loner in his neighborhood, you're fucked. Plus, he's been dealing since the second grade, so those guys must have went after him when he was only about seven years old. The pros like to use real little kids because they can shove them through windows and doors that don't open real far, plus if some little kid gets caught, the cops can't throw him in jail or beat him up to make him squeal.

For about two seconds, I really thought T.J. was going to cut me. Then for another second I thought he was going to kiss me, or at least hug me, but then all of a sudden he jerked his hand back and cracked his fist across the top of my head.

He must have knocked me out because the next thing I knew, I was sitting on that bench and Tío was handing me my books and saying, "What happened?" but I said I didn't remember. I had a cut on my neck, not too deep, but a lot of blood on my shirt. Everybody thinks I got mugged by some meth addict and they all feel sorry for me except Primo who thinks I'll look cool with a scar on my neck. But T.J. is the one I feel sorry for because he doesn't even know he has a choice. He really believes he has to be a loser forever.

Today, I got my letters from Lupe, so I'm glad I believed in her and didn't let T.J. put a bad idea into my head. But I still wish I could erase that half of a second when I wasn't sure.

CHAPTER 26

VEINTE-VEINTE VISION

ONE MORE WEEK AND SCHOOL WILL BE OVER AND I'LL GO BACK to Rosablanca and my old life. I started to think what if as soon as I get back there, I start messing up again and go back to being a loser. But Lupe says the real losers are the people who are too afraid to try and see what they can be. So I'm going to try real hard because even though there are some advantages to being a juvenile delinquent—like most of the teachers don't call on you because they don't expect you to know anything, and some really hot girls like badass guys— you always have to watch your back 24-7. And even though you get a rush from doing stuff like just walking up on the street and asking some old Anglo guy what time is it and he gives you his watch because he thinks you'll kill him or something, you get a different kind of rush from having people clap real loud and whistle when you read a poem that you wrote. And when somebody walks up to you after and says, "Dude, that was so hot you're smokin'," it feels pretty good even if the guy is a old hippie with a white ponytail and a tie-dye T-shirt. And who could complain about having a bunch of grown-up ladies tell you that you're handsome and charming and they aren't even your family.

Ramona even asked me did I want to join a writers' group where her and some other people meet at the Black Cat and share the stuff they are writing and tell each other what sucks and what's good, but I'm not sure I could do that. It might feel too weird to let people read my poems before they're done and what if I couldn't write any more good ones? But sometimes it's good to do things that feel weird because after you do them a little bit, they feel all right, like if you have to wear hard shoes for a wedding or something at first you miss your tennis shoes but after a while you forget about your feet and you can dance better because those hard shoes are more slippery plus if you got a killer suit to wear you could wreck the whole thing and look so lame if you wore some old dirty sneakers. So if I lived here I probably would try to be in the writer's group and see if it started to feel normal after a while except it would probably still feel weird if I told some old person that their poems sucked. I wouldn't say *sucked*, I would say they stunk or something nice like that, but it would still be weird because they're an old person and you're supposed to respect them if you can. But I couldn't join that group anyway because I'm going back to Rosablanca which is where I belong at least for right now.

I almost wish I could stay in T or C, even though I miss Lupe and Jaime and my family because I got used to writing a letter to Lupe every day and getting a letter from her every day, too. And I got used to how quiet it is with no TV so you have to go outside and appreciate nature instead. Some days when I walk by the river I get a feeling like I *am* the river, *El Rio Eduardo,* and I flow from here to *México,* full of fish and broken sticks and ducks and plastic bags and soda cans that the tourists throw into me because their brains are on vacation, too. I'm going to miss the river and that blue heron and even the weird food that I got used to. Tío taught me how to cook a couple things like brown rice and stir-fry vegetables so I can make the same food like he does. He bought me a wok for a going-away present. I bet I'll be the only Mexican kid in town who has his own wok. I can even eat with chopsticks, too, and now I know why Jenny Chu is so skinny.

I'll miss going to the Black Cat, too, and talking to Rhonda and letting Mr. Poe eat my shoelaces. But I'm going to keep working on my poems so when I come visit Tío I'll have something real good to read. I need some real good poems because now I got a new reputation to maintain. Last Sunday, I got up way early in the morning and went down to the river and wrote a poem in my new journal that Tío bought me for another going-away present. I thought it was a pretty good poem so I took it to the Black Cat except I chickened out and didn't sign up to read. I just sat there holding my journal with my poems in it, thinking that maybe next year I would come back and read something. But all of a sudden, the guy with the goatee said, "We have a new reader this week and his name is Eduardo Corazon. So please give him a warm welcome."

Everybody started clapping and looking at me and I felt like running out the door but I was sitting too far away and there were so many people I would have to jump over them or step on their feet. Ramona was sitting beside me and she put her hand on my arm and said, "Don't be mad, but I signed you up, honeybun." She touched my journal. "I could just feel whatever you got written in that there little book is burning up the pages, trying to get out into the world." Then she stood up and held out her hand and after a couple seconds I took it and she walked me up to the front and leaned over and kissed me on the cheek. "That's for good luck." When Ramona kissed me, this old guy named Gino who wears a hat like Columbo hollered, "I need some good luck, too!" and took off his hat and put it over his heart.

"Let's hear it, kid," Gino said, and everybody got real quiet. It's a good thing I had my journal because my hands were shaking so much that if I had my poem on a piece of paper it would have rattled so loud nobody could hear me. My journal shook a little bit but it didn't make any noise, so my voice came out real loud and it didn't squeak even once like it always used to do which is why I never read out loud in school. While I was reading my poem, in the back of my mind I was surprised because my voice sounded real deep and low, just the way my father sounds. My poem is mostly English with a little Spanish mixed in to spice it up, and it has a bilingual title: *"Veinte-Veinte* Vision" which means "Twenty-Twenty Vision" in case you only know English.

VEINTE-VEINTE VISION

If you don't like your life
you can open a book and follow the words to
    some new place
far far away from you where you can forget
that you are your father's heart attack and your
    mother's tears
and you walk with your eyes looking in
so you won't see yourself in the mirror
because you're afraid to look out at *el mundo*
in case there's no place for you in it

Or if you don't like your life
you could create your own book
and follow your own words to some new place
where you write yourself a new life
that makes your parents so proud they shine
    when they call you *mijo*

and you walk with your eyes looking out
so you can see yourself *con ojos abiertos y claros*
and you aren't afraid to look out at the world
because you made your own place in it

and even if the book of your life is a regular
    everyday story
and not a big bestselling *estrella*
you will still be glad you wrote every word
with your own mind
in your own blood
from your own *corazón*

When I finished reading my poem, the old hippie with the white ponytail stood up and whistled and everybody clapped and clapped so loud that my ears are still full of that noise, like the sound of a blue heron flying right up past your head into the sunrise until it is so high you can't hear it anymore. You just see it floating in the air like a giant gray feather while *el sol* smiles down on the cactus-covered banks of the Rio Grande and makes *todo el mundo* shine like gold.

Ay te watcho.

ACKNOWLEDGMENTS

Muchas gracias to Rhonda and the Black Cat poets who adopted Eddie as their own emerging poet, and to all the teachers and counselors who listened to bits of his story and encouraged me to continue writing. Special thanks to Kevan Lyon for loving Eddie enough to whisk him off to New York to meet the publishers, and to Michelle Frey, every author's dream editor. A heartfelt hug to friends, writers, and former students for their advice and unwavering support, especially Susan Miranda, Terry Cummings, Mike Chavez, Dottie Ramowski, Renoly Santiago, Oscar Guerra, Rachel Fimbres, Lonnie Rubio, Alex González, Carlos Rodriguez, Dolores Bishop, Joanne Montoya, Marianne and "Butch" Thompson, Garland Bills, Cathy Henderson Martin, Barbara and Gary Asteak, Mary Ellen Boyling, Harley Shaw, Catherine and Betty Wanek, and Joan Neller.

LouAnne Johnson has been a U.S. Navy journalist, a Marine Corps officer, and a high school teacher. Her work with teens who were disenchanted with learning inspired her to write the memoir *My Posse Don't Do Homework*, which later became the major motion picture *Dangerous Minds*, starring Michelle Pfeiffer. LouAnne frequently speaks to educators around the country about her experiences in teaching and motivating teens to accomplish their dreams—and about how best to make schools work for kids.

LouAnne is currently traveling with her dog, Bogart. You can visit her on the Web at www.louannejohnson.com.